An Unspoken Hunger

Also by Terry Tempest Williams

The Secret Language of Snow (with Ted Major)
Pieces of White Shell
Between Cattails
Coyote's Canyon
Earthly Messengers
Refuge

An Unspoken Hunger

Stories from the Field

Terry Tempest Williams

Pantheon Books　　New York

*The essays in this work originally appeared in the following publications, whose editors I wish to thank for
their guidance:*

"In the Country of Grasses" in *The Norton Book of Nature Writing*, edited by Robert Finch
and John Elder, W. W. Norton, 1990; "In Cahoots With Coyote" in *The Faraway
Nearby: Georgia O'Keeffe as Icon*, Addison-Wesley Company, 1992; "Stone Creek
Woman" in *Elements*, Spring/Summer, 1992; "Winter Solstice at the Moab Slough" in
Three Essays: Bill McKibben, Terry Tempest Williams, William Least Heat Moon, Coffee House
Press, 1993; "An Unspoken Hunger" (as "Blood Relations") in *Northern Lights*, Winter,
1993; "A Eulogy for Edward Abbey" in *Journal of Energy, Natural Resources & Environmental
Law*, vol. 11, no. 1, 1990, University of Utah College of Law; "Yellowstone: The Erotics
of Place" in *High Country News*, June 3, 1991; "Mardy Murie: An Intimate Portrait" in
Patagonia, Spring 1991; "Testimony on Behalf of the Pacific Yew Act of 1991" in *Con-
gressional Record*, March 4, 1991; "The Architecture of a Soul" in *Orion*, Spring 1993;
"The Village Watchman" in *The Past of Friends*, edited by Mickey Pearlman, Houghton
Mifflin, 1994; "A Patriot's Journal" in *Witness*, vol. 5, no. 1, 1991; "All That Is Hidden"
in *Sierra*, March/April 1993; "Undressing the Bear" in *On Nature's Terms*, Texas A & M
University Press, 1992; "The Wild Card" in *Wilderness*, Summer, 1993; and "Redemp-
tion" in *Outside*, August 1993.

Permissions acknowledgments are on page 147.

Library of Congress Cataloging-in-Publication Data

Williams, Terry Tempest.
    An unspoken hunger : stories from the field / Terry Tempest
Williams.
        p.   cm.
    ISBN 0-679-43244-2
    I. Title.
    AC8.W653 1994
    081—dc20   93-30317

for
Callie, Sara, and Diane
with a prayer
for their future

So there was no going back: she had
to fight for survival among the mysteries
of life. And what human beings want
more than anything else is to become
human beings.

—Clarice Lispector,
An Apprenticeship

Contents

An Unspoken Hunger

In the
Country of Grasses

For a naturalist, traveling into unfamiliar territory is like turning a kaleidoscope ninety degrees. Suddenly, the colors and pieces of glass find a fresh arrangement. The light shifts, and you enter a new landscape in search of the order you know to be there.

As a naturalist who calls the Great Basin home, I entered the Serengeti Plains of Africa with beginner's eyes. The sky arched over me like a taut bow. George Schaller describes the Serengeti as "a boundless region with horizons so wide one can see clouds between the legs of an ostrich."

In the Country of Grasses

This is true. It is also true that the Serengeti ecosystem is defined by the hooves of migrating wildebeests. It covers the borders of Tanzania and Kenya like the stretched skin of an animal—25,000 square kilometers of open plains and wooded grasslands harbor one of the last refuges on earth where great herds of animals and their predators can wander at will.

I chose to wander in the northern appendage of these plains, in an area known as the Maasai Mara.

The Mara is wild, uninterrupted country capable of capturing one's spirit like cool water in a calabash. And it appears endless, as its southern boundary is contiguous with Tanzania's Serengeti National Park.

The Mara belongs to the Maasai or the Maasai to the Mara. The umbilical cord between man and earth has not been severed here. The Maasai pasture their cattle next to leopard and lion. They know the songs of grasses and the script of snakes. They move like thin shadows across the savannah. A warrior with a red cloak draped over his shoulder stands silhouetted against the sun. Beef-eaters, blood-drinkers, the Maasai are one of the last strongholds of nomadic life.

Samuel Kiplangat was my guide in the Mara. He is Maasai. The stretched holes in the lobes of his ears are like small windows and a reminder of the traditional life he has left behind. But he has not abandoned his native intelligence. Samuel felt the presence of animals long before he saw them. I watched him pull animals out of hiding with his eyes. I saw him penetrate stillness with his senses.

When traveling to new country, it is a gift to have a guide. They know the nuances of the world they live in. Samuel smells rain the night before it falls. I trust his instincts and borrow them until I uncover my own. But there is danger here. One can become lazy in the reliance on a guide. The burden of a newcomer is to pay attention.

The Land Rover slips into the savannah like a bird dog entering a marsh. We are fully present. I watch Samuel's eyes scan the horizon. He points south.

"Zebra," he says. "They are migrating north from Tanzania. Thousands more are on their way."

Hundreds of zebras walk the skyline. They become animated heat waves.

We drive closer. I have never seen such concentrations of animals. At one point I think I hear thunder. It is the hooves of wildebeests. Suddenly, the herd of zebra expands to include impalas, gazelles, and animals I do not recognize.

"Topi," Samuel says.

I flip through my field guide of African mammals and find it. An extraordinary creature, it is the color of mahogany with blue patches on its flanks and ocher legs. I look at the topi again, this time through binoculars. Its black linear face with spiraling horns creates the illusion of a primitive mask. The topi I watch stands motionless on a termite mound. Binoculars down, I look at Samuel. He says the topi resemble hartebeests. A small herd of topi runs in front of the vehicle in a rocking-horse gait and vanishes.

Samuel gives away his knowledge sparingly—in gentle, quiet doses. He is respectful of his teachers and those he is teaching. In this way he is generous. He gives me the pleasure of discovery. Slowly, African riddles unravel themselves like a piece of cut linen.

The sweet hissing of grasses accompanies us as we move ahead. We pass the swishing tails of wildebeests. We are looking for lions.

Anticipation is another gift for travelers in unfamiliar territory. It quickens the spirit. The contemplation of the unseen world; imagination piqued in consideration of animals.

We stop. Samuel points. I see nothing. I look at Samuel for clues. He points again. I still see nothing but tall, tawny grasses around the base of a lone tree. He smiles and says, "Lions."

I look. I look so hard it becomes an embarrassment—and then I see eyes. Lion eyes. Two amber beads with a brown matrix. Circles of contentment until I stand; the lion's eyes change, and I am flushed with fear.

"Quiet," Samuel whispers. "We will watch for a while."

As my eyes become acquainted with lion, I begin to distinguish fur from grass. I realize there are two lions, a male and a female lying together under the stingy shade of a thorn tree. I can hear them breathe. The male is breathing hard and fast, his black mane in rhythm with the breeze. He puts his right paw on the female's shoulder. Ears twitch. We are no more than ten feet away. He yawns. His yellow canines are as long as my index finger. His jowls look like well-worn leather. He stands. The grasses brush his belly. Veins protrude from his leg muscles. This lion is lean and strong. No wonder that in the Maasai mind every aspect of a lion is imbued with magic.

Acting oblivious to us, he moves to the other side of the tree. From the protection of the Land Rover, we spot a fresh kill. It is a wildebeest whose black flesh has been peeled back from a red scaffolding of bones. The lion sits on his haunches and feeds. He separates the wildebeest's legs with his paws and slowly sinks his teeth into the groin. He pulls and tears large strips of meat. With his head tilted, his carnassials shear more muscle and viscera from the body cavity. His rasping tongue licks the blood from the bones. Ribs snap. His claws clamp down on the wildebeest as though escape was still possible.

The carcass is like a cave that the lion enters. He growls, and the female joins him. He nibbles her ear and then licks her face and neck. I am startled by his blood-stained muzzle. Side by side, two lions devour their prey.

The sensuality of predator-prey relations is riveting. My Great Basin eyes transfer lion and wildebeest to mountain lion and mule deer. The guffawing hyena on the periphery of the pride becomes a coyote squinting through sage.

The wildebeest is smothered by the lion's paw. Who knows how long they will stay. Night falls, and beyond the pride of lions, hyenas jockey for their place among bones. Beyond hyenas, jackals pace. Finally, white-backed vultures clean the kill as ravens do in the desert. There is no such thing as waste except in the world of man. The concentric circles which bind a healthy habitat include vulnerable and venerable species.

It is a familiar scenario, predator and prey, as though a shaft of light falls in the forgotten corner of an attic, and a precious possession is retrieved. We too are predators. A primal memory is struck like a match.

I hold on to a rope between two poles. I grip with both hands the life I live and the one I have forgotten. When in the presence of natural order, we remember the potentiality of life, which has been overgrown by civilization.

Morning comes quickly near the equator. There is little delineation of dawn. On the Serengeti, it is either day or night. A peculiar lull occurs just before sunrise. The world is cool and still. Gradually, the sun climbs the ladder of clouds until the sky mirrors the nacreous hues of abalone.

Samuel tells us this morning we will look for rhinos. I dream of looking into the eyes of these creatures, but Samuel warns us our chances are few. There are only two rhinoceros in the region. Only two. Male and female.

No one speaks for some time. The isolation of endangered species is disquieting. Two rhinos. And in ten years what will the count be?

We drive toward Rhino Ridge. It is broken country—rugged, pocked, and gnarled. Volcanic boulders lie on the land like corpses of stone. Even if we don't see rhino, I say to myself, it is good to know where they live.

Samuel points out a dung heap around a small bush. Tracks surrounding the mound indicate spreading of the dung. A well-trodden path is also apparent. I later learn from Samuel that because rhinos are solitary and nomadic, they have a complex olfactory system of communication. These "lavatories" are an indirect means of keeping in touch.

I am fascinated by what Samuel sees and what I am missing. In the Great Basin I can read the landscape well. I know the subtleties of place. A horned lizard buried in the sand cannot miss my eyes, because I anticipate his. A kit fox at night streaks across the road. His identity is told by the beam of my headlights. And when a great horned owl hoots above my head, I hoot too. Home is the range of one's instincts.

In the Country of Grasses

As a naturalist, I yearn to extend my range like the nomadic lion, rhino, or Maasai. But in remote and unfamiliar territory, I must learn to read the landscape inch by inch. The grasses become braille as I run my fingers through them.

Samuel is listening. I listen too. My attention is splayed between hoopoes and hyenas. Suddenly, there is a rumbling. Samuel nods. Elephants. A herd of a dozen or more, young and old, thunder through the underbrush. Trunks flaring, waving up and down, ears fanning back and forth, tusks on the front end, tails at the rear. These were animals I had never imagined wild. As they pass, I focus on their skin. It is a landscape unto itself. The folds and creases in the hide become basin and range topography.

In the scheme of the savannah, the elephant breaks into forests and opens wooded country to the vegetation and animals of the plains. The rhino depends on the elephant to create a transition zone from woodlands to grasslands. Under natural conditions a new generation of elephants would migrate to another area and repeat the cycle of vegetative succession. But with man's encroachment there is not much space left for the emigration of elephants. The land becomes abused, and rhinos are left with less options for range. Even in Maasai Mara, whose appearance is primordial, natural equilibrium is shifting.

Samuel and I follow a brushfire. The smoke is a serpent winding down the Siria Escarpment. My eyes burn. Suddenly, Samuel freezes.

"Rhinos," he says. "Two rhinos."

Through the wildebeests, through the zebras, topi, and gazelles, I see two beasts the color of pewter moving quickly over the ridge. I guess them to be a mile away.

As we advance closer and closer, the anticipation of seeing rhinoceros is like crossing the threshold of a dream. The haze lifts and there they are—two rhinos, male and female, placidly eating grass with prehensile lips. Their skin is reminiscent of another time. It is the spirit of the animal that stands. Two rhinos, their eyes hidden in the folds of their armor. Oxpeckers perch on crescent horns. I catch the female's eye. She does not waver.

My vision blurs. Who would kill a rhinoceros? It seems clear that the true aphrodisiac is not found in their horns but in simply knowing they exist.

Only a few minutes of daylight remain. We leave. I look back one more time. From a distance, they have become outcroppings of stone. Two rhinos on the Serengeti Plains.

In *Out of Africa*, Isak Dinesen writes about what it means to be an outsider in Maasailand. She says, "I feel that it might altogether be described as the existence of a person who had come from a rushed and noisy world into still country."

We have forgotten what we can count on. The

natural world provides refuge. In the Great Basin, I know the sounds of strutting grouse and the season when sage blooms. A rattlesnake coiled around the base of greasewood is both a warning and a wonder. In Maasai Mara, marabou storks roost before sunset and baboons move in the morning. The dappled light on leaves may be a leopard in a tree. These are the patterns that awaken us to our surroundings. Each of us harbors a homeland, a landscape we naturally comprehend. By understanding the dependability of place, we can anchor ourselves as trees.

One night, Jonas Olé Sademaki, a Maasai elder, and I sit around the fire telling stories. Sparks enter the ebony sky and find their places among stars.

"My people worship trees," he says. "It was the tree that gave birth to the Maasai. Grasses are also trustworthy. When a boy is beaten for an inappropriate act, the boy falls to the ground and clutches a handful of grass. His elder takes this gesture as a sign of humility. The child remembers where the source of his power lies."

As I walk back to my tent, I stop and look up at the Southern Cross. These are new constellations for me. I kneel in the grasses and hold tight.

The Architecture
of a Soul

Pink murex. *Melongena corona*. Cowry. Conch. Mussel. Left-sided whelk. Lightning whelk. True-heart cockle. Olivella. Pribilof lora. Angel wings.

These are the names of shells, the shells my grandmother and I catalogued together during the winter of 1963. I was eight years old.

With field guides all around us, we thumbed through plates of photographs, identifying each shell. Mimi would read the descriptions out loud to be certain our classifications were correct. Then, with a blue ball-point pen, we would write the appropriate name on white adhesive tape and stick it on the corresponding shell.

"It's important to have a hobby," Mimi said, "something to possess you in your private hours."

My grandmother's hobby was spending time at the ocean, walking along the beach, picking up shells.

For a desert child, there was nothing more beautiful than shells. I loved their shapes, their colors. I cherished the way they felt in the palm of my hand—and they held the voice of the sea, a primal sound imprinted on me as a baby.

"Your mother and I took you to the beach shortly after you were born," Mimi said. "As you got older, you played in the sand by the hour."

I played with these shells in the bathtub. The pufferfish was my favorite animal. I knew it was dead, dried out, and hollow, but somehow when it floated in the hot water next to my small, pink body, it came to life—a spiny globe with eyes.

Mimi would knock on the bathroom door.

"Come in," I would say.

She surveyed my watery world. I handed her the puffer, wet.

"When I die," she said smiling, "these shells will be your inheritance."

Thirty years later, these shells—the same shells my grandmother collected on her solitary walks along the beach, the shells we spread out on the turquoise carpet of her study, the shells we catalogued, the shells I bathed with—now rest in a basket on a shelf in my study. They remind me of my natural history, that I was tutored by a woman who courted solitude and made pilgrimages to the edges of our continent in the name of her own pleasure, that beauty, awe, and curiosity were values illuminated in our own home.

My grandmother's contemplation of shells has become my own. Each shell is a whorl of creative expression, an architecture of a soul. I can hold *Melongena corona* to my ear and hear not only the ocean's voice, but the whisperings of my beloved teacher.

In Cahoots
with Coyote

Rumor has it, Georgia O'Keeffe was
walking in the desert; her long black skirt swept the sand.
She could smell bones. With palette and paintbrush in
hand, she walked west to find them.

It was high noon, hot, but O'Keeffe would not
be deterred. She walked down arroyos and up steep
slopes; her instincts were her guide. Ravens cavorted
above her, following this black-clothed creature through
the maze of juniper and sage.

Suddenly, O'Keeffe stopped. She saw bones. She
also saw Coyote and hid behind a piñon.

Coyote's yellow eyes burned like flames as he danced around the cow carcass with a femur in each hand. His lasso made of barbed wire had brought the bovine down. Maggots, beetles, and buzzards had miraculously cleaned the bones. The skull glistened. Coyote had succeeded once again. He had stripped the desert of another sacred cow.

Georgia stepped forward. Coyote stopped dancing. They struck a deal. She would agree not to expose him as the scoundrel he was, keeping his desert secrets safe, if he promised to save bones for her—bleached bones. Stones—smooth black stones would also do. And so, for the price of secrecy, anonymity, and just plain fun—O'Keeffe and Coyote became friends. Good friends. Through the years, he brought her bones and stones and Georgia O'Keeffe kept her word. She never painted Coyote. Instead, she embodied him.

Eliot Porter knew O'Keeffe as Trickster. It is a well-known story. I heard it from the photographer himself at a dinner party in Salt Lake City.

Porter told of traveling with Georgia into Glen Canyon, how much she loved the slickrock walls, and the hours she spent scouring the edges of the riverbed in search of stones.

"She was obsessed," he said, "very particular in what stones she would keep. They had to speak to her."

He paused. Grinned.

"But I was the one that found the perfectly black, perfectly round, perfectly smooth stone. I showed it to Georgia. She was furious that it was in my hands instead of hers. This stone not only spoke to her, it cried out and echoed off redrock walls!"

Porter smiled deviously.

"I didn't give it to her. I kept it for myself, saying it would be a gift for my wife, Aline.

"A few months later," Porter continued, "we invited Georgia to our home in Tesuque for Thanksgiving dinner. Aline and I knew how much Georgia loved that stone. We also knew her well enough to suspect she had not forgotten about it. And so we conducted an experiment. We set the black stone on our coffee table. O'Keeffe entered the room. Her eyes caught the stone. We disappeared into the kitchen to prepare the food, and when we returned, the stone was gone. Georgia said nothing. I said nothing. Neither did Aline. The next time I saw my black smooth stone, it was a photograph in *Life* magazine taken by John Loengard, in the palm of O'Keeffe's hand."

Georgia O'Keeffe had the ability to trick the public, as well as her friends. She seduced critics with her flowers, arousing sexual suspicion:

Well—I made you take time to look at what I saw and when you took time to really notice my flower you hung all your own associations with flowers on my flower and you write about my flower as if I think and see what you think and see of the flower—and I don't.

She transformed desert landscapes into emotional ones, using color and form to startle the senses. Scale belonged to the landscape of the imagination. When asked by friends if these places really existed, O'Keeffe responded with her usual candor, "I simply paint what I see."

What O'Keeffe saw was what O'Keeffe felt—in her own bones. Her brush strokes remind us again and again, nothing is as it appears: roads that seem to stand in the air like charmed snakes; a pelvis bone that becomes a gateway to the sky; another that is rendered like an angel; and "music translated into something for the eye."

O'Keeffe's eye caught other nuances besides the artistic. She was a woman painter among men. Although she resisted the call of gender separation and in many ways embodied an androgynous soul, she was not without political savvy and humor on the subject:

When I arrived at Lake George I painted a horse's skull—then another horse's skull and then another horse's skull. After that came a cow's skull on blue. In my Amarillo days cows had been so much a part of the country I couldn't think without them. As I was working I thought of the city men I had been seeing in the East. They talked so often of writing the Great American Novel—the Great American Play—the Great American

Poetry. I am not sure that they aspired to the Great American Painting. Cézanne was so much in the air that I think the Great American Painting didn't even seem a possible dream.

I knew cattle country—I was quite excited over our own country and I knew that at the time almost any one of those great minds would have been living in Europe if it had been possible for them. They didn't even want to live in New York—how was the Great American Thing going to happen? So as I painted along on my cow's skull on blue I thought to myself, "I'll make it an American painting. They will not think it great with the red stripes down the sides—Red, White and Blue—but they will notice it."

Georgia O'Keeffe had things to do in her own country and she knew it. She would bring the wanderlust men home, even to her beloved Southwest, by tricking them once again, into seeing the world her way, through bold color and the integrity of organic form. O'Keeffe's clarity would become the American art scene's confusion. The art of perception is deception—a lesson Coyote knows well.

Perhaps the beginning of O'Keeffe's communion with Coyote began in the Texas Panhandle. The year was 1916, the place Palo Duro Canyon. O'Keeffe saw this cut in the earth as "a burning, seething cauldron, almost like a blast furnace full of dramatic light and color."

Her pilgrimages to the canyon were frequent, often with her sister, Claudia. "Saturdays, right after breakfast we often drove the twenty miles to the Palo Duro Canyon. It was colorful—like a small Grand Canyon, but most of it only a mile wide. It was a place where few people went. . . . It was quiet down in the canyon. We saw the wind and snow blow across the slit in the plains as if the slit didn't exist."

She goes on to say:

The only paths were narrow, winding cow paths. There were sharp, high edges between long, soft earth banks so steep that you couldn't see the bottom. They made the canyon seem very deep. We took different paths from the edge so that we could climb down in new places. We sometimes had to go down together holding to a horizontal stick to keep one another from falling. It was usually very dry, and it was a lone place. We never met anyone there. Often as we were leaving, we would see a long line of cattle like black lace against the sunset sky.

Painting No. 21, *Palo Duro Canyon* (1916), celebrates an earth on fire, an artist's soul response to the dance of heat waves in the desert and the embrace one feels when standing at the bottom of a canyon with steep slopes of scree rising upward to touch a cobalt sky. It is as though O'Keeffe is standing with all her passion inside a red-hot circle with everything around her in motion.

And it is not without fear. O'Keeffe writes, "I'm frightened all the time . . . scared to death. But I've never let it stop me. Never!"

Once, after descending into a side canyon to look closely at the striations in the rock that resembled the multicolored petticoats of Spanish dancers, Georgia could contain herself no longer. She howled. Her companions, worried sick that she might have fallen, called to her to inquire about her safety. She was fine. Her response, "I can't help it—it's all so beautiful!"

I believe Coyote howled back.

O'Keeffe's watercolor *Canyon with Crows* (1917) creates a heartfelt wash of "her spiritual home," a country that elicits participation. The two crows (I believe they are ravens) flying above the green, blue, and magenta canyon are enjoying the same perspective of the desert below as the artist did while painting. O'Keeffe is the raven, uplifted and free from the urban life she left behind.

I had forgotten about Georgia O'Keeffe's roots in Palo Duro Canyon. I was traveling to Amarillo, Texas, for the first time in June 1988, to speak to a group of Mormons about the spirituality of nature. A woman in charge of the conference asked if I had any special needs.

"Just one," I replied. "We need to be outside."

What had originally been conceived as an indoor seminar was transformed into a camping trip. One hundred Mormons and I descended into Palo Duro Canyon in a rainstorm.

The country was familiar to me. It was more than reminiscent of my homeland. Certainly, the canyons of southern Utah are sisters to Palo Duro, but it was something else, a déjà vu, of sorts.

Cows hung on the red hillside between junipers and mesquite. I saw three new birds—a scaled quail, a golden-fronted woodpecker, and wild turkeys. Other birds were old friends: roadrunner, turkey vulture, scissor-tailed flycatcher, and rock wren. Burrowing owls stood their ground as mockingbirds threw their voices down-canyon, imitating all the others. It was a feathered landscape.

The Lighthouse, Spanish Dancers, and Sad Monkey Train were all landmarks of place. The bentonite hills were banded in ocher and mauve. Strange caves within the fickle rock looked like dark eyes in the desert, tears streaming from the rain.

We crossed three washes with a foot of water flowing through. Markers indicated that five feet was not unusual. Flash floods were frequent.

Mesquite had been brought in for a campfire. Food was being prepared. The rain stopped. The land dried quickly. A group of us sat on a hillside and watched the sun sink into the plains—a sun, large, round, and orange in a lavender sky.

At dusk, I knelt in the brown clay, dried and cracked, and rubbed it between my hands—a healing balm. Desert music of mourning doves and crickets began. Two ravens flew above the canyon. I looked up and suddenly remembered O'Keeffe. This was her country. Her watercolor *Canyon with Crows* came back to me. It was an animated canvas. I wondered if Georgia had knelt where I was, rubbing the same clay over her hands and arms as I was, some seventy years ago?

It was time for the fireside.

I stood in front of the burning mesquite with chalked arms and my *Book of Mormon* in hand. If I quoted a scripture first, whatever followed would be legitimate. This was important. The Priesthood leaders, men, had inquired about my status in the Church. When I replied, "Naturalist," they were not comforted.

I opened my scriptures and spoke of the earth, the desert, how nature mirrors our own. I began to read from the Doctrine and Covenants, section 88, verse 44— "And the Lord spoke . . ." when all at once, a pack of coyotes behind the rocks burst forth in a chorus of howls.

God's dogs.

I was so overcome with delight at the perfectness of this moment, I forgot all religious protocol and joined them. Throwing back my head, I howled too—and invited the congregation to do likewise—which they did. Mormons and coyotes, united together in a desert howl-lelujah chorus!

I said, "Amen." Silence was resumed and the fireside ended.

In Cahoots with Coyote

That night, we slept under stars. I overheard a conversation between two women.

"Did you think that was a little weird tonight?"

"I don't know," the other replied, "howling with the coyotes just seemed like the natural thing to do."

The Village
Watchman

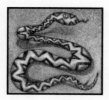

      Stories carved in cedar rise from the deep woods of Sitka. These totem poles are foreign to me, this vertical lineage of clans; Eagle, Raven, Wolf, and Salmon. The Tlingit craftsmen create a genealogy of the earth, a reminder of mentors, that we come into this world in need of proper instruction. I sit on the soft floor of this Alaskan forest and feel the presence of Other.

      The totem before me is called "Wolf Pole" by locals. The Village Watchman sits on top of Wolf's head with his knees drawn to his chest, his hands holding them tight against his body. He wears a red-and-black-striped hat. His eyes are direct, deep-set, painted blue. The expression on his face reminds me of a man I loved, a man who was born into this world feet first.

"Breech——" my mother told me of her brother's birth. "Alan was born feet first. As a result, his brain was denied oxygen. He is special."

As a child, this information impressed me. I remember thinking fish live underwater. Maybe Alan had gills, maybe he didn't need a face-first gulp of air like the rest of us. His sweet breath of initiation came in time, slowly moving up through the soles of his tiny webbed feet. The amniotic sea he had floated in for nine months delivered him with a fluid memory. He knew something. Other.

Wolf, who resides in the center of this totem, holds the tail of Salmon with his feet. The tongue of Wolf hangs down, blood-red, as do his front paws, black. Salmon, a sockeye, is poised downriver—a swish of a tail and he could be gone, but the clasp of Wolf is strong.

There is a story of a boy who was kidnapped from his village by the Salmon People. He was taken from his family to learn the ways of water. When he returned many years later to his home, he was recognized by his own as a Holy Man privy to the mysteries of the unseen world. Twenty years after my uncle's death, I wonder if Alan could have been that boy.

But our culture tells a different story, more alien

than those of Tlingit or Haida. My culture calls people
of sole-births retarded, handicapped, mentally disabled
or challenged. We see them for who they are not, rather
than for who they are.

My grandmother, Lettie Romney Dixon, wrote
in her journal, "It wasn't until Alan was sixteen months
old that a busy doctor cruelly broke the news to us. Others may have suspected our son's limitations but to those
of us who loved him so unquestionably, lightning struck
without warning. I hugged my sorrow to myself. I felt
abandoned and lost. I wouldn't accept the verdict. Then
we started the trips to a multitude of doctors. Most of
them were kind and explained that our child was like a
car without brakes, like an electric wire without insula-
tion. They gave us no hope for a normal life."

Normal. Latin: *normalis*; *norma*, a rule; conform-
ing with or constituting an accepted standard, model, or
pattern, especially corresponding to the median or aver-
age of a large group in type, appearance, achievement,
function, or development.

Alan was not normal. He was unique; one and
only; single; sole; unusual; extraordinary; rare. His emo-
tions were not measured, his curiosity not bridled. In a
sense, he was wild like a mustang in the desert and, like
most wild horses, he was eventually rounded up.

He was unpredictable. He created his own rules
and they changed from moment to moment. Alan was
twelve years old, hyperactive, mischievous, easily frus-

trated, and unable to learn in traditional ways. The situation was intensified by his seizures. Suddenly, without warning, he would stiffen like a rake, fall forward and crash to the ground, hitting his head. My grandparents could not keep him home any longer. They needed professional guidance and help. In 1957 they reluctantly placed their youngest child in an institution for handicapped children called the American Fork Training School. My grandmother's heart broke for the second time.

Once again, from her journal: "Many a night my pillow is wet from tears of sorrow and senseless dreamings of 'if things had only been different,' or wondering if he is tucked in snug and warm, if he is well and happy, if the wind still bothers him. . . ."

The wind may have continued to bother Alan, certainly the conditions he was living under were less than ideal, but as a family there was much about his private life we never knew. What we did know was that Alan had an enormous capacity for adaptation. We had no choice but to follow him.

I followed him for years.

Alan was ten years my senior. In my mind, growing up, he was mythic. Everything I was taught not to do, Alan did. We were taught to be polite, to not express displeasure or anger in public. Alan was sheer, physical expression. Whatever was on his mind was vocalized and usually punctuated with colorful speech. We would go bowling as a family on Sundays. Each of us would take our turn, hold the black ball to our chest, take a few steps, swing our arm back, forward, glide, and release— the ball would roll down the alley, hit a few pins, we would wait for the ball to return, and then take our second run. Little emotion was shown. When it was Alan's turn, it was an event. Nothing subtle. His style was Herculean. Big man. Big ball. Big roll. Big bang. Whether it was a strike or a gutter, he clapped his hands, spun around in the floor, slapped his thighs and cried, "Goddamn! Did you see that one? Send me another ball, sweet Jesus!" And the ball was always returned.

I could always count on my uncle for a straight answer. He was my mentor in understanding that one of the remarkable aspects of being human was to hold opposing views in our mind at once.

"How are you doing?" I would ask.

"Ask me how I am feeling?" he answered.

"Okay, how are you feeling?"

"Today? Right now?"

"Yes."

"I am very happy and very sad."

"How can you be both at the same time?" I asked in all seriousness, a girl of nine or ten.

"Because both require each other's company. They live in the same house. Didn't you know?"

We would laugh and then go on to another topic. Talking to my uncle was always like entering a maze of riddles. Ask a question. Answer with a question and see where it leads you.

My younger brother Steve and I spent a lot of time with Alan. He offered us shelter from the conventionality of a Mormon family. At our home during Christmas, he would direct us in his own nativity plays. "More—" he would say to us, making wide gestures with his hands. "Give me more of yourself." He was not like anyone we knew. In a culture where we were taught socially to be seen not heard, Alan was our mirror. We could be different too. His unquestioning belief in us as children, as human beings, was in startling contrast to the way we saw the public react to him. It hurt us. What we could never tell was if it hurt him.

Each week, Steve and I would accompany our grandparents south to visit Alan. It was an hour's drive to the training school from Salt Lake City, mostly through farmlands.

We would enter the grounds, pull into the parking lot of the institution where a playground filled with huge papier-mâché storybook figures stood (a twenty-foot pied piper, a pumpkin carriage with Cinderella inside, the old woman who lived in a shoe), and nine out of ten times, Alan would be standing outside his dormitory waiting for us. We would get out of the car and he would run toward us, throwing his powerful arms around us. His hugs cracked my back and at times I had to fight for my breath. My grandfather would calm him down by simply saying, "We're here, son. You can relax now."

Alan was a formidable man, now in his early twenties, stocky and strong. His head was large with a protruding forehead that bore many scars, a line-by-line history of seizures. He always had on someone else's clothes—a tweed jacket too small, brown pants too big, a striped golf shirt that didn't match. He showed us appearances didn't matter, personality did. If you didn't know him, he could look frightening. It was an unspoken rule in our family that the character of others was gauged in how they treated him. The only thing consistent about his attire was that he always wore a silver football helmet from Olympus High School where my grandfather was coach. It was a loving, practical solution to protect Alan when he fell. Quite simply, the helmet cradled his head and absorbed the shock of the seizures.

"Part of the team," my grandfather Sanky would say as he slapped him affectionately on the back. "You're a Titan, son, and I love you—you're a real player on our team."

The windows to the dormitory were dark, reflecting Mount Timpanogos to the east. It was hard to see inside, but I knew what the interior held. It looked like an abandoned gymnasium without bleachers, filled with hospital beds. The stained white walls and yellow-waxed floors offered no warmth to its residents. The stench was nauseating, sweat and urine trapped in the oppression of stale air. I recall the dirty sheets, the lack of privacy, and the almond-eyed children who never rose from their beds. And then I would turn around and face Alan's cheerfulness, the open and loving manner in which he would introduce me to his friends, the pride he exhibited as he showed me around his home. I kept thinking, Doesn't he see how bad this is, how poorly they are being treated? His words would return to me, "I am very happy and I am very sad."

For my brother and me, Alan was our guide, our elder. He was fearless. But neither one of us will ever be able to escape the image of Alan kissing his parents goodbye after an afternoon with family and slowly walking back to his dormitory. Before we drove away, he would turn toward us, take off his silver helmet, and wave. The look on his face haunts me still. Alan walked point for all of us.

Alan liked to talk about God. Perhaps it was in these private conversations that our real friendship was forged.

"I know Him," he would say when all the adults were gone.

"You do?" I asked.

"I talk to Him every day."

"How so?"

"I talk to Him in my prayers. I listen and then I hear His voice."

"What does He tell you?"

"He tells me to be patient. He tells me to be kind. He tells me that He loves me."

In Mormon culture, children are baptized a member of the Church of Jesus Christ of Latter-Day Saints when they turn eight years old. Alan had never been baptized because my grandparents believed it should be his choice, not something simply taken for granted. When he turned twenty-two, he expressed a sincere desire to join the Church. A date was set immediately.

The entire Dixon clan convened in the Lehi Chapel, a few miles north of the group home where Alan was now living. We were there to support and witness his conversion. As we walked toward the meetinghouse where this sacred rite was to be performed, Alan had a violent seizure. My grandfather and Uncle Don, Alan's elder brother, dropped down with him, holding his head and body as every muscle thrashed on the pavement like a school of netted fish brought on deck. I didn't want to look, but to walk away would have been worse. We stayed with him, all of us.

"Talk to God," I heard myself saying under my breath. "I love you, Alan."

"Can you hear me, darling?" It was my grand-mother's voice, her hand holding her son's hand.

By now, many of us were gathered on our knees around him, our trembling hands on his rigid body.

The Village Watchman

And we, who have always thought
Of happiness as rising, would feel
The emotion that almost overwhelms us
Whenever a happy thing falls.
                    —*Rainer Maria Rilke*

Alan opened his eyes. "I want to be baptized," he said. The men helped him to his feet. The gash on his left temple was deep. Blood dripped down the side of his face. He would forgo stitches once again. My mother had her arm around my grandmother's waist. Shaken, we all followed him inside.

Alan's father and brother ministered to him, stopped the bleeding and bandaged the pressure wound, then helped him change into the designated white garments for baptism. He entered the room with great dignity and sat on the front pew with a dozen or more eight-year-old children seated on either side. Row after row of family sat behind him.

"Alan Romney Dixon." His name was called by the presiding bishop. Alan rose from the pew and met his brother Don, also dressed in white, who took his hand and led him down the blue-tiled stairs into the baptismal font filled with water. They faced the congregation. Don raised his right arm to the square in the gesture of a holy oath as Alan placed his hands on his brother's left forearm. The sacred prayer was offered in the name of the Father, the Son, and the Holy Ghost, after which my uncle put his right hand behind Alan's shoulder and gently lowered him into the water for a complete baptism by immersion.

Alan emerged from the holy waters like an angel.

The breaking away of childhood
Left you intact. In a moment,
You stood there, as if completed
In a miracle, all at once.
    —*Rainer Maria Rilke*

Six years later, I found myself sitting in a chair across from my uncle at the University Hospital, where he was being treated for a severe ear infection. I was eighteen. He was twenty-eight.

"Alan," I asked. "What is it really like to be inside your body?"

He crossed his legs and placed both hands on the arms of the chair. His brown eyes were piercing.

"I can't tell you what it's like except to say I feel pain for not being seen as the person I am."

A few days later, Alan died alone; unique; one and only; single; in American Fork, Utah.

The Village Watchman sits on top of his totem with Wolf and Salmon—it is beginning to rain in the forest. I find it curious that this spot in southeast Alaska has brought me back into relation with my uncle, this man of sole-birth who came into the world feet first. He reminds me of what it means to live and love with a broken heart; how nothing is sacred, how everything is sacred. He was a weather vane—a storm and a clearing at once.

Shortly after his death, Alan appeared to me in a dream. We were standing in my grandmother's kitchen. He was leaning against the white stove with his arms folded.

"Look at me, now, Terry," he said smiling. "I'm normal—perfectly normal." And then he laughed. We both laughed.

He handed me his silver football helmet that was resting on the counter, kissed me, and opened the back door.

"Do you recognize who I am?"

On this day in Sitka, I remember.

Water Songs

Lee Milner and I stood in front of the diorama of the black-crowned night heron at the American Museum of Natural History in New York City. *Nycticorax nycticorax*: a long-legged bird common in freshwater marshes, swamps, and tidal flats, ranging from Canada to South America.

We each had our own stories. My tales were of night herons at the Bear River Migratory Bird Refuge in Utah—the way they fly with their heads sunken in line with their backs, their toes barely projecting beyond their tail, the way they roost in trees with their dark green feathered robes. Lee painted them at Pelham Bay Park on the northern edge of the Bronx, where, she says, "they fly about you like moths." Both of us could re-create their steady wingbeats with our hands as they move through crepuscular hours.

Two women, one from Utah and one from the Bronx, brought together by birds.

We were also colleagues at the American Museum. I was there as part of an exchange program from the Utah Museum of Natural History, on staff for six weeks. Lee was hired to manage the Alexander M. White Natural Science Center while the program director was on medical leave. The center is a special hands-on exhibit where children can learn about nature in New York City.

We worked together each day, teaching various school groups about the natural history in and around their neighborhoods. In between the toad, turtle, and salamander feedings, we found time to talk. Lee was passionate about her home. She would pull out maps of Pelham Bay Park and run her fingers over every slough, every clump of cattails and stretch of beach that was part of this ecosystem. She would gesture with her body the way the light shifts, exposing herons, bitterns, and owls. And she spoke with sadness about being misunderstood, how people outside the Bronx did not recognize the beauty.

I wasn't sure I did.

Lee and her father had just moved to Co-op City, and she described the view from their apartment as perfect for looking out over cattails. She promised to take me to Pelham Bay before I left.

The opportunity finally came. Our aquarium had been having bacteria problems that had killed some of the organisms. We decided we could use some more intertidal creatures: crabs, shrimps, and maybe some barnacles. We needed to go collecting. Pelham Bay was the place.

David Spencer, another instructor, agreed to come along. The plan was to meet Lee at Co-op City in the morning. David and I packed our pails, nets, and collecting gear before leaving the museum for the bus. Our directions were simple—one crosstown transfer, a few blocks up, and we were on the Fordham Road bus to Co-op City.

The idea of finding anything natural in the built environment passing my window seemed unnatural. All I could see was building after building, and beyond that, mere shells of buildings burnt out and vacant with empty lots mirroring the human deprivation.

"South Bronx," remarked David as he looked out his window.

Two elderly women sitting across from us, wrapped in oversized wool coats, their knees slightly apart, smiled at me. I looked down at my rubber boots with my old khakis tucked inside, my binoculars around

my neck and the large net I was holding in the aisle—
how odd I must look. I was about to explain, when their
eyes returned to their hands folded neatly across their
laps. I asked David, who was reading, if he felt the slightest bit silly or self-conscious.

"No," he said. "Nothing surprises New York-
ers." He returned to his book.

We arrived at Co-op City. Lee was there to meet
us. I was not prepared for the isolating presence of these
high-rise complexes that seemed to grow out of the
wetlands. Any notion of community would have to be
vertical.

From her apartment, Lee had a splendid view of
the marshes. Through the haze, I recognized the Empire
State Building and the twin towers of the World Trade
Center. The juxtaposition of concrete and wetlands was
unsettling, as they did nothing to inspire each other.

"The water songs of the red-winged blackbirds
are what keep me here," Lee said as we walked toward
Pelham Bay. "I listen to them each morning before I take
the train into the city. These open lands hold my sanity."

"Do other tenants of Co-op City look at the
marsh this way?" David asked.

"Most of them don't see the marsh at all," she
replied.

I was trying hard not to let the pristine marshes I
knew back home interfere with what was before us. The
cattails were tattered and limp. Water stained with oil

swirled around the stalks. It smelled of sewage. Our wetlands are becoming urban wastelands. This one, at least,
had not completely been dredged, drained, or filled.

It was midwinter, with an overcast sky. The
mood was sinister. But I trusted Lee, and the deeper we
entered into Pelham Bay Park, the more hauntingly beautiful it became, in spite of the long shadows and thin sil-
houettes of men behind bushes.

"This is a good place for us to collect," she said,
putting down her bucket at the estuary.

Within minutes, we were knee-deep in tide
pools and sloughs. My work was hampered by the ensu-
ing muck that leached into the water. I could not see,
much less find, what one would naturally assume to be
there. More oil slicks. Iridescent water. Yellow foam. I
kept coming up with gnarled oysters with abnormal
growths on their shells. I handed an oyster dripping with
black ooze to David.

"Eat this," I said.

"Not until you lick off your fingers first," he replied, wiping the animal clean.

These wetlands did not sparkle and sing. They
were moribund.

Lee didn't see them this way. She knew too
much to be defensive, yet recognized her place as their
defender, the beauty inherent in marshes as systems of
regeneration. She walked toward us with a bucket of
killifish, some hermit crabs, and one ghost shrimp.

"Did you see the night heron?" she asked.

I had not seen anything but my own fears fly by with a few gulls.

We followed her through a thicket of hardwoods to another clearing. She motioned us down in the grasses.

"See him?" she whispered.

On the edge of the rushes stood the black-crowned night heron. Perfectly still. His long white plumes, like the misplaced hairs of an old man, hung down from the back of his head, undulating in the breeze. We could see his red eye reflected in the slow, rippling water.

Lee Milner's gaze through her apartment window out over the cattails was not unlike the heron's. It will be this stalwartness in the face of terror that offers wetlands their only hope. When she motioned us down in the grasses to observe the black-crowned night heron still fishing at dusk, she was showing us the implacable focus of those who dwell there.

This is our first clue to residency.

Somehow, I felt more at home. Seeing the heron oriented me. I relaxed. We watched the mysterious bird until he finally outpatienced us. We left to collect a few more organisms before dark.

I made a slight detour. I wanted to walk on the beach during sunset. There was no one around. The beach was desolate, with the exception of a pavilion. It

stood on the sand like a forgotten fortress. Graffiti looking more like Japanese characters than profanities
streaked the walls. The windows, without glass, appeared
as holes in a decaying edifice. In the middle of the prome-
nade was a beautiful mosaic sundial. Someone had cared
about this place.

In spite of the cold, I took off my boots and
stockings and rolled up the cuffs of my pants. I needed to
feel the sand and the surf beneath my feet. The setting
sun looked like the tip of a burning cigarette through the
fog. Up ahead, a black body lay stiff on the beach. It was
a Labrador. Small waves rocked the dead dog back and
forth. I turned away.

Lee and David were sitting on the pavilion stairs
watching more night herons crisscross the sky. Darkness
was settling in. Lee surmised we had wandered a good six
miles or so inside the park. Even she did not think we
should walk back to Co-op City after sunset. They had
found a phone booth while I was out walking and had
called a cab.

"So are we being picked up here?" I asked.

They looked at each other and shook their
heads.

"We have a problem," David said. "No one will
come get us."

"What do you mean?"

"The first company we dialed thought we were a
prank call," said Lee. "Sure, you're out at Pelham Bay.

Sure ya'll want a ride into the city. No cabby in hell's dumb enough to fall for that one . . . click."

"And the second company hung up on us," David said. "At least the third cab operation offered us an alternative. They said our only real option was to call for a registered car."

"Let's do it," I said.

"We would have except we've run out of change," Lee replied.

I handed her what I had in my pockets. She called a gypsy cab service.

Waiting for our hired car's headlights to appear inside this dark urban wilderness was the longest thirty minutes I can remember. We stood on the concrete steps of the pavilion like statues, no one saying a word. I thought to myself, We could be in Greece, we could be in a movie, we could be dead.

The registered car slowly pulled up and stopped. The driver pushed the passenger's door open with his foot. Because of all our gear, I sat in front. Our driver could barely focus on our faces, let alone speak. I noticed his arms ravaged with needle tracks, how his entire body shook.

Eight silent miles. Thirty dollars. I gave him a generous tip and later felt guilty, knowing where the money would go. David and I hugged Lee, thanked her, and took the specimens, buckets, screens, and nets with us as we caught the bus back to Manhattan. The hour-long ride back to the city allowed me to settle into my fatigue. I dreamed of the pavilion, the stiff black dog, and the long-legged birds who live there.

David tapped me on the shoulder. I awoke startled. Disoriented.

"Next stop is ours," he said.

We got off the bus and walked over to Madison and Seventy-ninth Street to catch the crosstown bus back to the museum. We kept checking the fish to see if they were safe, surprised to see them surviving at all given the amount of sloshing that had occurred throughout the day.

As we stood on the corner waiting, a woman stopped. "Excuse me," she said. "I like your look. Do you mind me asking you where you purchased your trousers and boots? And the binoculars are a fabulous accessory."

I looked at David, who was grinning.

"Utah," I said in a tired voice. "I bought them all in Utah."

"I see . . ." the woman replied. "I don't know that shop." She quickly disappeared into a gourmet deli.

Back at the museum, the killifish were transferred safely into the aquarium with the shrimp and crabs. Before we left, I placed the oysters in their own tank for observation. With our faces to the glass, we watched the aquariums for a few minutes to make certain all was in order. Life appeared fluid. We turned off the lights and left. In the hallway, we heard music. Cocktail chatter. It was a fund-raising gala in the African Hall. We quietly slipped out. No one saw us enter or leave.

Walking home on 77th Street, I became melancholy. I wasn't sure why. Usually, after a day in the field I am exhilarated. I kept thinking about Lee, who responds to Pelham Bay Park as a lover, who rejects this open space as a wicked edge for undesirables, a dumping ground for toxins or occasional bodies. Pelham Bay is her home, the landscape she naturally comprehends, a sanctuary she holds inside her unguarded heart. And suddenly, the water songs of the red-winged blackbirds returned to me, the songs that keep her attentive in a city that has little memory of wildness.

Erosion

In 1910, Tsuru and Kinji Kurumada left Japan and immigrated to Richfield, Utah. Kinji Kurumada was a farmer. He loved the Utah soil, which yielded robust harvests of potatoes, tomatoes, melons, and corn. Day after day, he worked the land. But perhaps Mr. Kurumada was best known for his canyon lettuce and for how he supplied neighboring counties each year with his greens. There were family priorities. Each spring, the lettuce was planted way into the night, as it had to be harvested before the Fourth of July. The moon would shine. The seeds would be folded into the earth. And as ritual would have it for more than thirty years, the canyon lettuce grew and was harvested early, just as the community had come to expect, year after year.

Mr. Kurumada also had an uncanny gift for recognizing soils. It grew out of his intimacy with the land. It was a game with residents, bringing the old man samples. They would hold out their hands, dirt in both palms, and ask, "Where are these from?"

He would look at them, mull them over in his own fingers, and then reply, "This is from Monroe Mountain—and this soil belongs to Capitol Reef."

And then other locals would come forth with two more handfuls. The old man would make a clod from the loose dirt. "Glacial till. Draper, Utah. And this—looks like Big Cottonwood Canyon."

He was usually right. Kinji Kurumada knew his ground, establishing a firm "sense of place" for himself and his family.

In the spring—March 15, 1942, to be exact—June Kurumada, son of Kinji Kurumada, was on a bus for California. He was traveling with members of the Japanese-American Citizens' League. The bus was stopped. June was pulled off, arrested, and jailed. It was the beginning of the process of interning Japanese-Americans in camps.

Had Kinji Kurumada been around to check the soils, he would have found two handfuls: one from Topaz, Utah; the other from Heart Mountain, Wyoming.

Undressing the Bear

       He came home from the war and shot a bear. He had been part of the Tenth Mountain Division that fought on Mount Belvedere in Italy during World War II. When he returned home to Wyoming, he could hardly wait to get back to the wilderness. It was fall, the hunting season. He would enact the ritual of man against animal once again. A black bear crossed the meadow. The man fixed his scope on the bear and pulled the trigger. The bear screamed. He brought down his rifle and found himself shaking. This had never happened before. He walked over to the warm beast, now dead, and placed his hand on its shoulder. Setting his gun down, he pulled out his buck knife and began skinning the bear that he would pack out on his horse. As he pulled the fur coat away from the muscle, down the breasts and over the swell of the hips, he suddenly stopped. This was not a bear. It was a woman.

Another bear story: There is a woman who travels by sled dogs in Alaska. On one of her journeys through the interior, she stopped to visit an old friend, a Koyukon man. They spoke for some time about the old ways of his people. She listened until it was time for her to go. As she was harnessing her dogs, he offered one piece of advice.

"If you should run into Bear, lift up your parka and show him you are a woman."

And another: I have a friend who manages a bookstore. A regular customer dropped by to browse. They began sharing stories, which led to a discussion of dreams. My friend shared hers.

"I dreamt I was in Yellowstone. A grizzly, upright, was walking toward me. Frightened at first, I began to pull away, when suddenly a mantle of calm came over me. I walked toward the bear and we embraced."

The man across the counter listened, and then said matter-of-factly, "Get over it."

*   *   *

Why? Why should we give up the dream of embracing the bear? For me, it has everything to do with undressing, exposing, and embracing the Feminine.

I see the Feminine defined as a reconnection to the Self, a commitment to the wildness within—our instincts, our capacity to create and destroy; our hunger for connection as well as sovereignty, interdependence and independence, at once. We are taught not to trust our own experience.

The Feminine teaches us experience is our way back home, the psychic bridge that spans rational and intuitive waters. To embrace the Feminine is to embrace paradox. Paradox preserves mystery, and mystery inspires belief.

I believe in the power of Bear.

The Feminine has long been linked to the bear through mythology. The Greek goddess Artemis, whose name means "bear," embodies the wisdom of the wild. Christine Downing, in her book *The Goddess: Mythological Images of the Feminine*, describes her as "the one who knows each tree by its bark or leaf or fruit, each beast by its footprint or spoor, each bird by its plumage or call or nest."

It is Artemis, perhaps originally a Cretan goddess of fertility, who denounces the world of patriarchy, demanding chastity from her female attendants. Callisto, having violated her virginity and become pregnant, is transformed into the She-Bear of the night sky by

Artemis. Other mythical accounts credit Artemis herself as Ursa Major, ruler of the heavens and protectress of the Pole Star or *axis mundi*.

I saw Ursa Major presiding over Dark Canyon in the remote corner of southeastern Utah. She climbed the desert sky as a jeweled bear following her tracks around the North Star, as she does year after year, honoring the power of seasonal renewal.

At dawn, the sky bear disappeared and I found myself walking down-canyon. Three years ago, the pilgrimage had been aborted. I fell. Head to stone, I rolled down the steep talus slope stopped only by the grace of an old juniper tree precariously perched at a forty-five-degree angle. When I stood up, it was a bloody red landscape. Placing my hand on my forehead, I felt along the three-inch tear of skin down to the bony plate of my skull. I had opened my third eye. Unknowingly, this was what I had come for. It had been only a few months since the death of my mother. I had been unable to cry. On this day, I did.

Now scarred by experience, I returned to Dark Canyon determined to complete my descent into the heart of the desert. Although I had fears of falling again, a different woman inhabited my body. There had been a deepening of self through time. My mother's death had become part of me. She had always worn a small silver bear fetish around her neck to keep her safe. Before she died, she took off the bear and placed it in my hand. I wore it on this trip.

In canyon country, you pick your own path. Walking in wilderness becomes a meditation. I followed a small drainage up one of the benches. Lithic scatter was everywhere, evidence of Anasazi culture, a thousand years past. I believed the flakes of chert and obsidian would lead me to ruins. I walked intuitively. A smell of cut wood seized me. I looked up. Before me stood a lightning-struck tree blown apart by the force of the bolt. A fallout of wood chips littered the land in a hundred-foot radius. The piñon pine was still smoldering.

My companion, who came to the burning tree by way of another route, picked up a piece of the charred wood, sacred to the Hopi, and began carving a bull-roarer. As he whirled it above our heads on twisted cordage, it wailed in low, deep tones. Rain began—female rain falling gently, softly, as a fine mist over the desert.

Hours later, we made camp. All at once, we heard a roar up-canyon. Thunder? Too sustained. Jets overhead? A clear sky above. A peculiar organic smell reached us on the wind. We got the message. Flushed with fear, we ran to higher ground. Suddenly, a ten-foot wall of water came storming down the canyon, filling the empty streambed. If the flood had struck earlier, when we were hiking in the narrows, we would have been swept away like the cottonwood trees it was now carrying. We watched the muddy river as though it were a parade, continually inching back as the water eroded the earth beneath our feet.

That night, a lunar rainbow arched over Dark Canyon like a pathway of souls. I had heard the Navajos speak of them for years, never knowing if such magic could exist. It was a sweep of stardust within pastel bands of light—pink, lavender, yellow, and blue. And I felt the presence of angels, even my mother, her wings spread above me like a hovering dove.

In these moments, I felt innocent and wild, privy to secrets and gifts exchanged only in nature. I was the tree, split open by change. I was the flood, bursting through grief. I was the rainbow at night, dancing in darkness. Hands on the earth, I closed my eyes and remembered where the source of my power lies. My connection to the natural world is my connection to self—erotic, mysterious, and whole.

The next morning, I walked to the edge of the wash, shed my clothes, and bathed in pumpkin-colored water. It was to be one of the last warm days of autumn. Standing naked in the sand, I noticed bear tracks. Bending down, I gently placed my right hand inside the fresh paw print.

Women and bears.

Marian Engel, in her novel *Bear*, portrays a woman and a bear in an erotics of place. It doesn't matter whether the bear is seen as male or female. The relationship between the two is sensual, wild.

The woman says, "Bear, take me to the bottom of the ocean with you, Bear, swim with me, Bear, put your arms around me, enclose me, swim, down, down, down, with me."

"Bear," she says suddenly, "come dance with me."

They make love. Afterward, "She felt pain, but it was a dear sweet pain that belonged not to mental suffering, but to the earth."

I have felt the pain that arises from a recognition of beauty, pain we hold when we remember what we are connected to and the delicacy of our relations. It is this tenderness born out of a connection to place that fuels my writing. Writing becomes an act of compassion toward life, the life we so often refuse to see because if we look too closely or feel too deeply, there may be no end to our suffering. But words empower us, move us beyond our suffering, and set us free. This is the sorcery of literature. We are healed by our stories.

By undressing, exposing, and embracing the bear, we undress, expose, and embrace our authentic selves. Stripped free from society's oughts and shoulds, we emerge as emancipated beings. The bear is free to roam.

If we choose to follow the bear, we will be saved from a distractive and domesticated life. The bear becomes our mentor. We must journey out, so that we might journey in. The bear mother enters the earth before snowfall and dreams herself through winter, emerging in spring with young by her side. She not only survives the barren months, she gives birth. She is the caretaker of the unseen world. As a writer and a woman with obligations to both family and community, I have tried to adopt this ritual in the balancing of a public and private life. We are at home in the deserts and mountains, as well as in our dens. Above ground in the abundance of spring and summer, I am available. Below ground in the deepening of autumn and winter, I am not. I need hibernation in order to create.

We are creatures of paradox, women and bears, two animals that are enormously unpredictable, hence our mystery. Perhaps the fear of bears and the fear of women lies in our refusal to be tamed, the impulses we arouse and the forces we represent.

Last spring, our family was in Yellowstone. We were hiking along Pelican Creek, which separated us from an island of lodgepole pines. All at once, a dark form stood in front of the forest on a patch of snow. It was a grizzly, and behind her, two cubs. Suddenly, the sow turned and bolted through the trees. A female elk crashed through the timber to the other side of the clearing, stopped, and swung back toward the bear. Within seconds, the grizzly emerged with an elk calf secure in the grip of her jaws. The sow shook the yearling violently by the nape of its neck, threw it down, clamped her claws on its shoulders, and began tearing the flesh back from the bones with her teeth. The cow elk, only a few feet away, watched the sow devour her calf. She pawed the earth desperately with her front hooves, but the bear was oblivious. Blood dripped from the sow's muzzle. The cubs stood by their mother, who eventually turned the carcass over to them. Two hours passed. The sow buried the calf for a later meal, she slept on top of the mound with a paw on each cub. It was not until then that the elk crossed the river in retreat.

We are capable of harboring both these responses to life in the relentless power of our love. As women connected to the earth, we are nurturing and we are fierce, we are wicked and we are sublime. The full range is ours. We hold the moon in our bellies and fire in our hearts. We bleed. We give milk. We are the mothers of first words. These words grow. They are our children. They are our stories and our poems.

By allowing ourselves to undress, expose, and embrace the Feminine, we commit our vulnerabilities not to fear but to courage—the courage that allows us to write on behalf of the earth, on behalf of ourselves.

Winter Solstice
at the Moab Slough

It is the shortest day of the year. It is also the darkest. Winter Solstice at the Moab Slough is serene. I am here as an act of faith, believing the sun has completed the southern end of its journey and is now contemplating its return toward light.

A few hundred miles south, the Hopi celebrate Soyálangwul, "the time to establish life anew for all the world."

At dawn, they will take their prayer sticks, páhos, to a shrine on the edge of the mesa and plant them securely in the earth. The páhos, decorated with feathers, will make prayers to the sun, the moon, the fields, and the orchards. These prayer feathers will call forth blessings of health and love and a fullness of life for human beings and animals.

And for four days, the Hopi will return to their shrine and repeat the prayers of their hearts.

My heart finds openings in these wetlands, particularly in winter. It is quiet and cold. The heat of the summer has been absorbed into the core of the redrocks. Most of the 150 species of birds that frequent these marshes have migrated. Snowy egrets and avocets have followed their instincts south. The cattails and bulrushes are brittle and brown. Sheets of ice become windowpanes to another world below. And I find myself being mentored by the land once again, as two great blue herons fly over me. Their wingbeats are slow, so slow they remind me that, all around, energy is being conserved. I too can bring my breath down to dwell in a deeper place where my blood-soul restores to my body what society has drained and dredged away.

Even in winter, these wetlands nourish me.

I recall the last time I stood here near the Solstice—June 1991. The Moab Slough was christened the Scott M. Matheson Wetland Preserve. The Nature Conservancy set aside over eight hundred acres in the name of wildness.

A community gathered beneath blue skies in celebration of this oasis in the desert, this oxbow of diversity alongside the Colorado River. A yellow and white tent was erected for shade as we listened to our elders.

"A place of renewal . . ." Mrs. Norma Matheson proclaimed as she honored her husband, our governor of Utah, whose death and life will be remembered here, his name a touchstone for a conservation ethic in the American West.

"A geography of hope . . ." Wallace Stegner echoed. "That these delicate lands have survived the people who exploited this community is a miracle in itself."

We stood strong and resolute as neighbors, friends, and family witnessed the release of a red-tailed hawk. Wounded, now healed, we caught a glimpse of our own wild nature soaring above willows. The hawk flew west with strong, rapid wingbeats, heartbeats, and I squinted in the afternoon sun, following her with my eyes until she disappeared against the sandstone cliffs.

Later, I found a small striated feather lying on the ground and carried it home, a reminder of who we live among.

D. H. Lawrence writes, "In every living thing there is a desire for love, for the relationship of unison with the rest of things."

I think of my own stream of desires, how cautious I have become with love. It is a vulnerable enterprise to feel deeply and I may not survive my affections. André Breton says, "Hardly anyone dares to face with open eyes the great delights of love."

If I choose not to become attached to nouns—a

person, place, or thing—then when I refuse an intimate's love or hoard my spirit, when a known landscape is bought, sold, and developed, chained or grazed to a stubble, or a hawk is shot and hung by its feet on a barbed-wire fence, my heart cannot be broken because I never risked giving it away.

But what kind of impoverishment is this to withhold emotion, to restrain our passionate nature in the face of a generous life just to appease our fears? A man or woman whose mind reins in the heart when the body sings desperately for connection can only expect more isolation and greater ecological disease. Our lack of intimacy with each other is in direct proportion to our lack of intimacy with the land. We have taken our love inside and abandoned the wild.

Audre Lorde tells us, "We have been raised to fear the yes within ourselves . . . our deepest cravings. And the fear of our deepest cravings keeps them suspect, keeps us docile and loyal and obedient, and leads us to settle for or accept many facets of our own oppression."

The two herons who flew over me have now landed downriver. I do not believe they are fearful of love. I do not believe their decisions are based on a terror of loss. They are not docile, loyal, or obedient. They are engaged in a rich, biological context, completely present. They are feathered Buddhas casting blue shadows on the snow, fishing on the shortest day of the year.

Páhos. Prayer feathers. Darkness, now light. The

Winter Solstice turns in us, turns in me. Let me plant my own prayer stick firmly in the mud of this marsh. Eight hundred acres of wetlands. It is nothing. It is everything. We are a tribe of fractured individuals who can now only celebrate remnants of wildness. One red-tailed hawk. Two great blue herons.

Wildlands' and wildlives' oppression lies in our desire to control and our desire to control has robbed us of feeling. Our rib cages have been broken and our hearts cut out. The knives of our priests are bloody. We, the people. Our own hands are bloody.

"Blood knowledge," says D. H. Lawrence. "Oh, what a catastrophe for man when he cut himself off from the rhythm of the year, from his unison with the sun and the earth. Oh, what a catastrophe, what a maiming of love when it was made a personal, merely personal feeling, taken away from the rising and setting of the sun, and cut off from the magical connection of the solstice and equinox. This is what is wrong with us. We are bleeding at the roots. . . ."

The land is love. Love is what we fear. To disengage from the earth is our own oppression. I stand on the edge of these wetlands, a place of renewal, an oasis in the desert, as an act of faith, believing the sun has completed the southern end of its journey and is now contemplating its return toward light.

Stone Creek Woman

Few know her, but she is always there—Stone Creek Woman—watching over the Colorado River.

Over the years, I have made pilgrimages to her, descending into the Grand Canyon, passing through geologic layers with names like Kayenta, Moenave, Chinle, Shinarump, Toroweep, Coconino, and Supai to guide me down the stone staircase of time. It is always a pleasant journey downriver to Mile 132—Stone Creek, a small tributary that flows into the Colorado. We secure our boats and meander up the side canyon where the heat of the day seeps into our skin, threatens to boil our blood, and we can imagine ourselves as lizards pushing up and down on the hot, coral sand. They watch us step from stone to stone along the streambed. The lizards vanish and then we see her. Stone Creek Woman: guardian of the desert with her redrock face, maidenhair ferns, and waterfall of expression. Moss, the color of emeralds, drapes across her breasts.

I discovered her by accident. My husband, Brooke, and I were with a group on a river trip. It was high noon in June. Twice that morning the boatman had mentioned Stone Creek and what a refuge it would be: the waterfall, the shade-filled canyon; the constant breeze; the deep green pool. Searing heat inspired many of us to jump off the boats before they had been tied down. The group ran up Stone Creek in search of the enchanted pool at the base of the waterfall, leaving me behind.

I sauntered up Stone Creek. Sweat poured off my forehead and I savored the salt on my lips. The dry heat reverberated off the canyon's narrow walls. I relished the sensation of being baked. I walked even more slowly, aware of the cicadas, their drone that held the pulse of the desert. An evening primrose bloomed. I knelt down and peeked inside yellow petals. The pistil and stamens resembled stars. My index finger brushed them, gently, and I inhaled pollen. No act seemed too extravagant in

these extreme temperatures. Even the canyon wren's joy-
ous anthem, each falling note, was slow, full, and luxuri-
ous. In this heat, nothing was rushed.

Except humans.

Up ahead, I heard laughter, splashing, and the
raucous play of friends. I turned the corner and found
them bathing, swimming, and sunning. It was a kaleidoscope of color. Lycra bodies, some fat, some thin, sun-
burned, forgetting all manner of self-consciousness. They
were drunk with pleasure.

I sat on a slab of sandstone near the edge of the
pool with my knees pulled into my chest and watched,
mesmerized by the throbbing waterfall at Stone Creek,
its sudden surges of energy, how the moss anchored on
the redrock cliff became neon in sunlight, how the long
green strands resembled hair, how the fine spray rising
from the water nurtured rainbows.

I eventually outwaited everyone. As Brooke led
them back to the boats, the glance we exchanged told me
I had a few precious moments I could steal for myself.
And in that time, I shed my clothing like snakeskin. I
swam beneath the waterfall, felt its pelting massage on
my back, stood up behind it, turned and touched the
moss, the ferns, the slippery rock wall. No place else
to be.

I sank into the pool and floated momentarily on
my back. The waterfall became my focus once again.
Suddenly, I began to see a face emerging from behind the

veil of water. Stone Creek Woman. I stood. I listened to her voice.

Since that hot June day, I have made a commitment to visit Stone Creek Woman as often as I can. I believe she monitors the floods and droughts of the Colorado Plateau, and I believe she can remind us that water in the West is never to be taken for granted. When the water flows over the sandstone wall, through the moss and the ferns, she reveals herself. When there is no water, she disappears.

For more than five million years, the Colorado River has been sculpting the Grand Canyon. Stone Creek, as a small tributary to the Colorado, plays its own role in this geologic scheme. The formation I know as Stone Creek Woman has witnessed these changes. The Colorado River, once in the soul-service of cutting through rocks, is now truncated by ten major dams generating twelve million kilowatts of electricity each year. Red water once blessed with sediments from Glen Canyon is now sterile and blue. Cows drink it. We drink it. And crops must be watered. By the time twenty million people in seven western states quench their individual thirsts and hose down two million acres of farmland for their food, the Colorado River barely trickles into the Gulf of California.

If at all.

Water in the American West is blood. Rivers, streams, creeks, become arteries, veins, capillaries. Dam, dike, or drain any of them and somewhere, silence prevails. No water: no fish. No water: no plants. No water: no life. Nothing breathes. The land-body becomes a corpse. Stone Creek Woman crumbles and blows away.

Deserts are defined by their dryness, heat, and austerity of form. It is a landscape best described not by what it is, but by what it is not.

It is not green.

It is not lush.

It is not habitable.

Stone Creek Woman knows otherwise. Where there is water, the desert is verdant. Hanging gardens on slickrock walls weep generously with columbines, monkey flowers, and mertensia. A thunderstorm begins to drum. Lightning dances above the mesa. Clouds split. Surging rain scours canyons in a flash of flood. An hour later, there is a clearing. Potholes in the sandstone become basins to drink from. Creatures—coyote, kit fox, rattlesnake, mule deer—adapted to the call of aridity, drink freely, filling themselves from this temporary abundance. Stone Creek Woman begins to dance.

I want to join them.

Wallace Stegner, in his book *The Sound of Mountain Water*, says, "In this country you cannot raise your eyes without looking a hundred miles. You can hear coyotes who have somehow escaped the air-dropped poison baits designed to exterminate them. You can see in every sandy pocket the pug tracks of wildcats, and every water pocket in the rock will give you a look backward into geologic time, for every such hole swarms with triangular crablike creatures locally called tadpoles but actually first cousins to the trilobites who left their fossil skeletons in the Paleozoic."

And here stands Stone Creek Woman, guardian and gauge of the desert, overlooking the Colorado River, with her redrock face, her maidenhair ferns, and waterfall of expression. I have found a handful of people who have seen her. There may be more. Some say she cannot speak. Others will tell you she is only to be imagined. But in the solitude of that side canyon where I swam at her feet, she reminds me we must stand vigilant.

A Eulogy
for Edward Abbey

Arches National Park
May 20, 1989

We are a family, a tribe, a clan,
flocked together at a full moon in May, on slickrock. We
have made a pilgrimage to the center of the universe,
Abbey's country. Things are different now. Edward
Abbey is gone. We know the physical fact of these words
and we grieve. We know the spiritual truth of the words
and we smile. Ed is here and will always be. His words
reverberate on canyon walls, his voice being carried by
desert winds on the open skies of the American West. He
is Coyote, a dance upon the desert.

A Eulogy for Edward Abbey

Edward Abbey didn't have to die to find paradise. He understood and lived it here and now. His words:

When I write paradise, I mean not apple trees and only golden women, but also scorpions and tarantulas and flies, rattlesnakes and gila monsters, sandstone, volcanos, and earthquakes, bacteria, bear, cactus, yucca, bladderweed, ocotillo and mesquite, flash floods and quicksand, and yes, disease and death and the rotting of flesh. Paradise is the here and now, the actual, tangible dogmatically real Earth on which we stand. Yes, God bless America, the Earth upon which we stand.

Abbey knew we had it all right here, right now, we need not look farther, we need not go further. Ed's death lay on surfaces. His words:

For my own part, I am pleased enough with surfaces. In fact, they alone seem to be of much importance. Such things for example as the grasp of a child's hand in your own, the flavor of an apple, the embrace of a friend or lover, the silk of a girl's thigh, the sunlight on rock and leaves, the feel of music, the bark of a tree, the abrasion of granite and sand, the plunge of clear water into a pool, the face of the wind, what else is there, what else do we need?

Perhaps there is one thing—I believe Ed knew and understood the art, the practice, of keeping in touch.

The simple act of correspondence. Familiar? One white, generic postcard from Wolf's Hole, from Oracle, from Moab, Utah. Signed always, "Love, Ed." Think about the thousands of postcards with Abbey's words, his scribblings that have crossed these lands, these sacred lands like a blizzard, like migrating birds, like shooting stars, U.S. Mail, Abbey's courier, keeping in touch.

I first received mine in October 1979. It read simply: "Nice meeting you in Salt Lake City, Tempest. Come to Tucson. I would like to show you around the desert. Love, Ed." The cards kept coming over the years, not often, but consistently. Small exchanges back and forth, simple jottings, a dialogue of news as well as ideas, keeping in touch.

A couple of autumns ago, September 1987, to be exact, Ed did show me the desert. Not in Tucson, but in Utah. His heartland, my homeland. We met in Moab; we spent the day in Millcreek Canyon. A simple meander through slickrock. I hear his voice ahead of me as we descend into the canyon, dropping from ledge to ledge: "What most humans really desire is really something quite different from industrial gimmickry—liberty, spontaneity, nakedness, mystery, wildness, wilderness." A Coors six-pack carton had lodged itself behind a bitterbrush. Abbey kicked it, bent down, set it on fire, kept walking. I hear his words: "What we need now are heroes and heroines, about a million of them, one brave deed is worth a thousand books. Sentiment without action is the ruin of the soul." We descend further into the canyon, jump a few more ledges. My confidence had been lost a few months earlier in a fall in Blacksteer Canyon, now called "Bumsteer Canyon." Eighty stitches running down the center of my forehead like a river. "So I hear you're trying to etch the Colorado Plateau on your face, Tempest," he kidded me. "Better make sure your words are as tough as your skin." I have not forgotten that. His words, tough as skin, are loyal to the earth, the earth that bore us and sustains us, the only home we shall ever know.

The rest of the day was spent sitting in pools, climbing in and out of alcoves, simply walking across desert meadows of prickly pears, globe mallows and cow pies. The same cow pies that fueled the *Moab Times Independent* with letters to the editors after his call for "no more cows, period!"

Abbey's humor solicited mine. We told stories. We walked in silence, just walked sharing the small wonders of the day in gentle conversation, in spirited debate. His gifts of listening, of asking the poignant questions, the barbs, the generosities . . . this strong, tall desert of a man, both shy and fierce, reflective and combative, in love with his public and in revolt against them. This human being of complex paradox and passion who lured us out of complacency again and again. I hear his voice:

Delicate arch, a fragile ring of stone. If it holds any significance, it lay in the power of the odd and unexpected

to startle the senses and surprise the mind out of their ruts
of habit, to compel us into a reawakened sense of the
wonderful.

Ed could have been talking about himself. With
Abbey, anything was possible, hence his seduction. His
broad smile, his big, old hands, his unforgettable voice
and cadence—that was the last time I walked with him.
The postcards kept coming, like a blizzard, like migrating birds, like shooting stars, keeping in touch.

Last week, I went back through Millcreek Canyon, retraced our steps through slickrock, recalled the
potholes that brought us to our knees, the light dancing
on redrock walls, the soft sand, that beloved pink sand
under boot, and the turkey vultures that always seemed to
circle him with fondness, with preference—who could
blame them for their possessive eye?

Things are different now. That's why we're here.
Change is growth, growth is life, and life is death. We are
here to honor Ed, to honor Clarke, Becky and Ben, Suzy,
Aaron and Josh, the Cartwrights, Howard and Nancy
Abbey; to acknowledge family, tribe, and clan. And it has
everything to do with love: loving each other, loving the
land. This is a rededication of purpose and place.

The canyons of southern Utah are giving birth to the
Coyote Clan—hundreds, maybe even thousands of

individuals who are quietly subversive on behalf of the land. And they are infiltrating our neighborhoods in the most respectable ways, with their long, bushy tails tucked discreetly inside their pants or beneath their skirts.

Members of the Clan are not easily identified, but there are clues. You can see it in their eyes. They are joyful and they are fierce. They can cry louder and laugh harder than anyone on the planet. And they have enormous range.

The Coyote Clan is a raucous bunch: they have drunk from desert potholes and belched forth toads. They tell stories with such virtuosity that you'll swear you have been in the presence of preachers.

The Coyote Clan is also serene. They can float on their backs down the length of any river or lose entire afternoons in the contemplation of stone.

Members of the Clan court risk and will dance on slickrock as flash floods erode the ground beneath their feet. It doesn't matter. They understand the earth re-creates itself day after day. . . .

One last promise, Ed: we shall go forth with a vengeance.

A full moon is rising. Howl and wait for his echo. Abbey's voice. I hear it. "Feet on earth, knock on wood, touch stone, good luck to all."

And may I add, keep in touch—with Ed, with each other, and with the earth.

Love always, the Earth.

An Unspoken Hunger

It is an unspoken hunger we deflect with knives—one avocado between us, cut neatly in half, twisted then separated from the large wooden pit. With the green fleshy boats in hand, we slice vertical strips from one end to the other. Vegetable planks. We smother the avocado with salsa, hot chiles at noon in the desert. We look at each other and smile, eating avocados with sharp silver blades, risking the blood of our tongues repeatedly.

Yellowstone:
The Erotics of Place

Steam rising. Water boiling. Geysers surging. Mud pots gurgling. Herds breathing. Hooves stampeding. Wings flocking. Sky darkening. Clouds gathering. Rain falling. Rivers raging. Lakes rising. Lightning striking. Trees burning. Thunder clapping. Smoke clearing. Eyes staring.

We call its name—and the land calls back.

Yellowstone.

Echo System.

Echo.

An echo is a sound wave that bounces back, or is reflected from, a large hard surface like the face of a cliff, or the flanks of a mountain, or the interior of a cave. To hear an echo, one must be at least seventeen meters or fifty-six feet away from the reflecting surface.

Echos are real—not imaginary.

We call out—and the land calls back. It is our interaction with the ecosystem; the Echo System.

We understand it intellectually.

We respond to it emotionally—joyously.

When was the last time we played with Echo?

The Greek god Pan played with her all the time.

Echo was a nymph and she was beautiful—long, dark hair flowing over her bare shoulders, lavender eyes, burnished skin and red lips. Pan was intrigued. He was god of wild nature—rustic, lustful, and seductive. But with his goat legs and horns, he could not woo Echo. She remained aloof, indifferent to his advances.

Pan was not accustomed to loving nymphs in vain. He struck her dumb, save for the power of repetition.

Echo roamed the woods and pastures repeating what she heard. The shepherds became incensed and seized her. They tore her body to pieces.

Gaia, the Earth Mother, quietly picked up the pieces of Echo and hid them in herself—where they still retain their repetitive powers.

Pan, seeking no further revenge, strengthened his vows to love the land in all its wildness—dancing in the woods, in the fields and grottoes, on mountaintops and in glens—dancing, chasing, and seducing the vulnerable, all in the name of fertility.

Pan, as we know him, is therianthropic—half-man and half-animal—with a bare chest and the lower limbs of a goat. Two small horns rise from his head like lightning rods. He is blessed with the goat's prodigious agility and bestial passions. He wears a crown made of pine boughs and blows through pipes of reed.

He is a dangerous creature.

But we know Pan is dead. Elizabeth Barrett Browning has told us so:

> Earth outgrows the mythic fancies
> Sung beside her in her youth . . .
>   Pan, Pan is dead.

These lines are founded on an early Christian belief that when the heavenly hosts told the shepherds at Bethlehem of the birth of Christ, a deep groan was heard throughout Greece. Pan was dead.

When James Watt was asked what he feared most about environmentalists, his response was simple: "I fear they are pagans."

He is right to be fearful.

I would like to suggest Pan is not dead, that Echo lives in her repetitive world, in the cycles and circles of nature.

I would like even to suggest that the Greater

Yellowstone: The Erotics of Place

Yellowstone Ecosystem/Echo System is a Pansexual landscape. Of Pan. A landscape that loves bison, bear, elk, deer, moose, coyote, wolf, rabbit, badger, marmot, squirrel, swan, crane, eagle, raven, pelican, red-tail, buf-flehead, goldeneye, teal, and merganser.

Pansexual. Of Pan. A landscape that loves white pine, limber pine, lodgepole, Douglas fir, blue spruce, aspen, cottonwood, willow, sage, serviceberry, huckle-berry, chokecherry, lupine, larkspur, monkshood, steershead, glacier lilies, spring beauties, bistort, and paintbrush.

Pansexual. Of Pan. A landscape where the Bitter-root Valley, the Sawtooths, Tetons, Wind Rivers, and Absarokas loom large in our imaginations—where Henry's Fork, the Clark Fork, the Snake, and the Mis-souri nourish us, refresh us, and revive our souls.

It is time for us to take off our masks, to step out from behind our personas—whatever they might be: educators, activists, biologists, geologists, writers, farm-ers, ranchers, and bureaucrats—and admit we are lovers, engaged in an erotics of place. Loving the land. Honoring its mysteries. Acknowledging, embracing the spirit of place—there is nothing more legitimate and there is nothing more true.

That is why we are here. It is why we do what we do. There is nothing intellectual about it. We love the land. It is a primal affair.

Pagans? Perhaps.

Involved in an erotics of place? Most definitely.

There are rituals along the way. Doug Peacock writes in *Grizzly Years*:

Before leaving for Bitter Creek, I had one more job to do: hide the head of the bull bison, which died in the open. If the Park Service discovers the head, rangers with sledgehammers are sent to smash the skull to pieces. This is to protect the bones from horn and head hunters, who spot the skull—perhaps from a helicopter—swoop down, pluck it up, and sell it to buyers who grind up every last piece of bone and antler for sale on the Asian market as an aphrodisiac.

Late in the morning, I packed up for Bitter Creek wondering where I should hide the bull buffalo head. He should have stayed where he was forever. Barring that, I thought he should rejoin the bull herd of about a dozen bison with which he spent his adult life. I had been looking after this herd for years, and stashed other skulls when bulls died during hard winters. He would join his buddies in a semicircle of four bison skulls facing the rising sun. A mile away, hidden where they would never be discovered, below trees and under the snow, I brought together a ghost herd of bison skulls, decorated with the feathers of crane and eagle, the recipients of bundles of sage and handfuls of earth carried from sacred mountains and offered up in private ceremonies.

Rituals. Ceremonies. Engaging with the land. Loving the land and dreaming it. An erotics of place.

Biologist Tim Clark says at the heart of good biology is a central core of imagination. It is the basis for responsible science. And it has everything to do with intimacy, spending time outside.

But we forget because we spend so much time inside—inside offices, inside boardrooms, inside universities, inside hearings, inside eating power breakfasts, power lunches, dinners, and drinks.

To protect what we love outside, we are inside scheming, talking, telephoning, writing, granting, faxing memos, memos, memos, memos to them, to us; inside to protect what we love outside.

There is no defense against an open heart and a supple body in dialogue with wildness. Internal strength is an absorption of the external landscape. We are informed by beauty, raw and sensual. Through an erotics of place our sensitivity becomes our sensibility.

If we ignore our connection to the land and disregard and deny our relationship to the Pansexual nature of earth, we will render ourselves impotent as a species. No passion—no hope of survival.

Edward Abbey writes, "Nature may be indifferent to our love, but never unfaithful."

We are a passionate people who are in the process of redefining our relationship toward the land.

And it is sensual.

I believe that out of an erotics of place, a politics of place is emerging. Not radical, but conservative, a politics rooted in empathy in which we extend our notion of community, as Aldo Leopold has urged, to include all life forms—plants, animals, rivers, and soils. The enterprise of conservation is a revolution, an evolution of the spirit.

We call to the land—and the land calls back.

Echo System.

Steam rising. Water boiling. Geysers surging. Mud pots gurgling. Herds breathing. Hooves stampeding. Wings flocking. Sky darkening. Clouds gathering. Rain falling. Rivers raging. Lakes rising. Lightning striking. Trees burning. Thunder clapping. Smoke clearing. Eyes staring. Wolves howling into the Yellowstone.

Mardy Murie

An Intimate Profile

 On June 5, 1977, in Denver, Colo-
rado, hundreds of individuals from the American West
gathered to testify on behalf of the Alaskan Lands Bill
sponsored by Representative Morris Udall. It was one of
the many regional hearings conducted by the House Interior Subcommittee on General Oversight and Alaskan
Lands.

Mardy Murie from Moose, Wyoming, was the
first to testify. She stood before the subcommittee and
said simply, "I am testifying as an emotional woman and

I would like to ask you, gentlemen, what's wrong with emotion?" She went on to say, "Beauty is a resource in and of itself. Alaska must be allowed to be Alaska, that is her greatest economy. I hope the United States of America is not so rich that she can afford to let these wildernesses pass by—or so poor she cannot afford to keep them."

The audience spontaneously gave Mrs. Olaus Murie a standing ovation. Her heartfelt words symbolized the long love affair she and her renowned biologist husband had shared with the Arctic.

I remember that day.

After the hearing, Mardy (whom I had met three years earlier at the Teton Science School) asked me if I had a ride home. I told her I was on my way back to Jackson Hole with Howie Wolke and Bart Kohler, at that time field reps for Friends of the Earth and The Wilderness Society.

"Good company," she said, smiling. "If those boys can defend the wilderness, they can defend you."

A few years later, "those boys," along with Dave Foreman, Mike Roselle, and Ron Kezar, would form Earth First!, making the cry with clenched fists, "No compromise in defense of Mother Earth."

In her maternal embrace of home, it is fair to say Mardy Murie was one of their mentors. Mardy Murie is certainly a mentor of mine. She is a woman who has exhibited—through her marriage, her children, her writing, and her activism—that a whole life is possible. Her commitment to relationships, both personal and wild, has fed, fueled, and inspired an entire conservation movement. She is our spiritual grandmother.

I recall an afternoon together in Moose. We drank tea in front of the stone hearth. A fire was crackling. It was snowing outside. She spoke of Olaus.

"We shared everything," she said. "Our relationship was a collaboration from the beginning. With Olaus employed by the Biological Survey (now the U.S. Fish and Wildlife Service), he was under contract to study caribou. We were married in Anvik, Alaska, on August 19, 1924. I had just graduated from the University of Alaska. We caught the last steamer north and spent our honeymoon on the Koyukuk River, which delivered us into the Brooks Range. Throughout the fall, we traveled the interior by dogsled, Olaus studying caribou all along the way. Those were magical days for us, and I loved living in the bush."

"How did your life change with children?" I asked.

"It didn't, really, we just took them with us. Our oldest son, Martin, was ten months old when Olaus accepted a contract to band geese on the Old Crow River. And after 1927, when we moved to Jackson Hole so Olaus could study the elk population, the children practically lived in the Teton wilderness."

She paused for a moment.

"The key was to plan well and have a solid base camp. I'd lash some tree limbs together for a table, and create a kitchen. Logs and stools and benches. The children adored being outside. They ran with their imaginations. And I never remember them being sick or cross. But the most marvelous thing of all, was that Olaus was always near. . . ."

Mardy refilled our cups of tea.

I looked at this silver-haired woman—so poised, so cultured—and marveled at her.

"So when did you begin writing?"

"I always kept a journal," she said. "But one day, Angus Cameron, a good friend of ours who was an editor at Knopf, encouraged me to write about the Alaska and Wyoming I knew. I just told our stories. My sense of wilderness is personal. It's the experience of being in wilderness that matters, the feeling of a place. . . ."

I told her how much *Two in the Far North* had influenced me as a young woman. I had read it shortly after Brooke and I were married, when we were traveling through Denali National Park. Here was an independent woman's voice rooted in family and landscape. "You trusted your instincts."

"I always have."

We paused. I was curious about so many aspects of her life, largely hidden now by her age of eighty-plus years.

"Olaus mentions 'one's place of enchantment' in *Wapiti Wilderness*. Where is yours?"

She looked out the window, but her gaze turned inward. "A certain bend in the river on the Sheenjek, a cock ptarmigan is sitting there. It's early summer. Mountains are in the background."

At that moment, the conversation shifted. "You know somebody has to be alert all the time. We must watch Congress daily. The Arctic National Wildlife Refuge is in such a precarious position right now, politically. All some people can see in these lands is oil, which means money, which translates into greed."

"Are you pessimistic?"

"I'm more apprehensive and at the same time more hopeful than I have ever been. I'm counting on the new generation coming up. I have to believe in their spirit, as those who came before me believed in mine.

"People in conservation are often stereotyped as solemn, studious sorts," Mardy went on. "It's not true. It's a community of people who are alive and passionate. My favorite photograph of Olaus is one where he is dancing with the Eskimo on Nunivak Island. You can see the light in his face and how much he is enjoying it. We always danced. It's how we coped with the long, dark winters.

"One year, after a particular arduous meeting, we took the members of the Governing Council of the Wilderness Society to Jenny Lake Lodge. We danced. A balance of cheerful incidents is good for people. If we allow ourselves to become discouraged, we lose our power and momentum."

She faced me directly. "That's what I would say to you, in the midst of these difficult times. If you are going into that place of intent to preserve the Arctic National Wildlife Refuge or the wildlands in Utah, you have to know how to dance."

There have been many more conversations with Mardy through the years, but what I love most about this woman is her warmth, her generosity of spirit, her modesty. "I just did the thing that seemed obvious doing." After Olaus' death from cancer in 1963, brokenhearted, but determined to live a happy life, Mardy made a commitment to continue with their collective vision of wilderness preservation and environmental education. She gave speeches to National Park Service officials, testimonies before Congress, and she has never forgotten the children. It has been in these years, almost three decades, that her voice has become her own with great heart, inspiration, and strength. Her leadership in the environmental movement is directly tied to her soul.

"My father said to me, 'If you take one step with all the knowledge you have, there is usually just enough light shining to show you the next step.' "

This past fall, I was with Mardy in Moose once again. The cottonwoods lining the gravel road to the log home where she and Olaus had lived since 1949 were blazing Teton gold. We sat on the couch together. We had our tea and caught up on one another's lives.

"I want to read you something, Terry." She disappeared into her bedroom and returned with a manuscript in hand. "This is part of a preface I am writing for a forthcoming book on Alaska."

Then she read:

There may be people who feel no need for nature. They are fortunate, perhaps. But for those of us who feel otherwise, who feel something is missing unless we can hike across land disturbed only by our footsteps or see creatures roaming freely as they have always done, we are sure there should be wilderness. Species other than man have rights, too. Having finished all the requisites of our proud, materialistic civilization, our neon-lit society, does nature, which is the basis for our existence, have the right to live on? Do we have enough reverence for life to concede to wilderness this right?

Our eyes met.

"Do you think we have it in us?" she asked.

A Patriot's Journal

"Is there any animal you would not kill?" I ask my uncle as we drive south from Salt Lake City to Las Vegas.

"Two," he answers. "A grizzly and a Siberian tiger."

"Why would you spare them?"

"Because they are so beautiful."

My uncle Richard Tempest and I are driving down to the Nevada Nuclear Test Site together in his silver Nissan 300ZX. Fourteen guns (one shotgun, eight rifles, and five pistols) with thirty boxes of ammunition lie in the backseat. I can feel the butt of a leather rifle case against my neck. There's not a lot of room in this car.

I notice the speedometer needle is moving past 75 mph. With one hand on the padded steering wheel, he points to the butte on our right.

"I've got private shooting galleries all across the West," he says. "I just pull off the road, set up some targets of cans, rocks, or whatever else I can find, and practice firing. If something live crosses in front of me, it's fair game. It relaxes me, gets my mind off work. I love Nevada."

I love my uncle, which is why I will not ask him any more questions for fear of what I may find out, like the numbers of coyotes, hawks, rabbits, and ravens he kills in any given week.

Hobbies, I think to myself—men and their hobbies.

I read Friday morning's paper out loud. The headline in the *Salt Lake Tribune* states, BUSH MAKES ONE LAST OFFER FOR TALKS TO PREVENT WAR.

Washington, D.C.—President Bush, facing deep divisions in Congress over war in the Persian Gulf, offered Thursday to send Secretary of State James Baker to Geneva for talks with Iraq's foreign minister in "one last attempt" at peace. . . . "No negotiations, no compromises, no attempts at face-saving and no rewards for aggression," Bush said.

Richard is accompanying his daughter, Lynne, her husband, Steve Earl, and me to the International Mass Demonstration and Nonviolent Direct Action scheduled for Saturday at the test site. The rally is sponsored by Greenpeace and American Peace Test.

"Why did you decide to come?" I asked my uncle.

"I'm curious," he said. "I want to see what you kids are up to. Besides, somebody has to bail you out if you get arrested."

Richard Tempest has been a state senator for the past four years. A Mormon conservative. Republican. A complex and sophisticated man. He is known for speaking his mind. His voting record is erratic: he sponsored a tire-recycling bill and pushed for clean-air legislation—but was against progressives on wilderness concerns and many social-reform bills.

He lost the last election to a Democrat heavily funded by the Utah Education Association, a real upset by Utah standards.

Lynne is the editor of *Network*, a feminist magazine. Steve is an engineer employed by Hercules. He designs hardware for the Space Shuttle and is having a difficult time with all the defense contracts that pass through his office.

Richard and I are to meet Lynne and Steve at the Mirage Hotel in Las Vegas. As we wait outside, the volcano erupts. Who knows how many thousand gallons of water are being used to pump this road show sky-high. Red lights create the illusion of molten lava. The crowd is impressed.

"How's Ruth feeling?" I ask. She completed chemotherapy for breast cancer in 1989.

"She's never felt better," he says. "But the fear of it coming back is with us all the time."

Lynne and Steve arrive.

"I want to show you something before we have dinner," he says.

We follow Richard through the lobby, past the shark tank, past the tropical jungle (a woman asks her husband if the orchids are real—"Only one way to tell," he says, "rip the petals and see"), through the casino to a glassed-in theater. Richard stops at the railing. Inside are two Siberian tigers asleep in front of a Rousseau-inspired tile mural. A couple standing next to us comment on how well the white tigers match the hotel decor. My uncle stares at the animals with great affection.

January 5, 1991

IRAQ, U.S. SET DATES FOR TALKS

Washington, D.C.—Iraq agreed Friday to hold its first high-level talks with the United States since it invaded

Kuwait, August 2. Baghdad tried anew to bring in the Palestinian issue but ran into a straight-arm from President Bush, who said, "There will be no linkage."

A photograph on the front page of the paper shows two airmen trudging through the windswept street of "Camel Lot," the nickname for an air base in central Saudi Arabia, home to 120 warplanes ready to bomb Iraqi targets.

We leave Las Vegas for the test site a little after dawn. The Strip is still lit, electric signs pulsating erotica and one-named stars like Elvis, Frank, Wayne, Cher. Doesn't matter if they are alive or dead. People pay.

"If God were to send down his first flicker of fire, it would be here," Richard says.

"Who needs God?" I retort.

Richard looks hard at me.

"We've done a pretty good job without him. Wait until you see the test site," I say.

Over fifty law enforcers dressed in desert fatigues stand guard.

We are standing in a prayer circle a few feet from the cattle guard that separates us from them. Step across that arbitrary line and you will be handcuffed and arrested.

A Maori woman begins to pray. Her voice is followed by Corbin Harney and Raymond Yowell,

Shoshone elders. This is the Shoshone sunrise ceremony. They pray to the Four Directions. A hundred or so people have gathered together. It evolves into a circle of testimonies, stories of why people have come. A woman from the Marshall Islands speaks: "All living things are dying on my island."

A Dominican sister from England, dressed in her black and white habit, says, "I am here out of guilt, out of anger and grief. My country tests here."

A Japanese film crew from Hiroshima has traveled many miles. One man steps forward. "We are recording the present, which might prevent the past from reoccurring."

A loaf of bread is passed around the circle. Each of us breaks off a piece and eats. I pass the loaf to my uncle. He is a spiritual man. He understands the idea of sacrament but did not anticipate this. Richard stands behind his aviator glasses, watching, his thumbs in the front pockets of his Levi's. He takes the bread, breaks it, and eats.

The bread continues around the circle, becoming smaller and smaller.

The rally begins. A stage has been constructed in the Mojave Desert. STOP NUCLEAR TESTING—PROTEST FOR NO TEST! Banners bearing the same message are written in Russian, Japanese, French, and Shoshone: "SHUNDAHAI," the Shoshone cry. Olzhas Suleimenov, a poet from Kazakhstan and a member of the Supreme Soviet, stands. He is a large man: impressive, Asian-looking, with long black curly hair. In February 1989, he initiated the Nevada-Semipalatinsk Movement and has come to the United States to consolidate public support for a comprehensive nuclear test ban.

Suleimenov was successful in stopping nuclear testing in Kazakhstan—Semipalatinsk is a nuclear test site similar to the one in Nevada—where his people have suffered cancer, sickness, and death from forty years of radioactive fallout. Now he wants the suffering to end for those living downwind of the Nevada Nuclear Test Site.

"Nevada and Kazakhstan are one and the same. We are living on the same earth. The threat is for all of us from all countries. No defense strategy justifies the actions of a government against its own people."

He speaks. The translator gives us his words.

"The point now should be to take care of life."

The crowd of almost three thousand cheers.

"The old Roman rule—if you want peace, prepare for war—has never worked. If we want peace, then we must prepare for peace."

The crowd cheers again. My uncle sits with us on a wooden bench close to the ground. I watch him tap the sand with his cowboy boots. The Soviet delegation is seated in front of us.

"Stop it!" Suleimenov cries. "Stop it! You don't have to touch the hearts of politicians; they are married to convention. It is the people who have hearts; they are the ones who carry the burden of political heartlessness.

The will of the Kazakhstan people was expressed simply and straightforwardly. We demanded that the Soviet government do what we wanted. You can demand the same thing. Stop it! Stop it!" He raises his open hand high. "Stop it!"

The crowd rises to its feet with the same gesture; a sea of open hands rises above our heads.

"Stop it! Stop it! Stop it!"

Suleimenov says, "We are voices uniting."

Next, Topa Merehau Raphael stands. He is a native activist with the Polynesian Liberation Front from Tahiti.

"I am not a prophet. I am not a messiah. I am like a small bird that has left a small boat to deliver an important message: Bombs are being tested off the shores of my island. My people are dying from radiation exposure. If we have a case to defend, it is not the case of the bomb—but the case of freedom and peace."

One of the four British women who spent three days walking toward Ground Zero at the Nevada Test Site undetected until minutes before a scheduled nuclear test rises on stage. Lorna. I did not catch her last name, as the crowd is deafening.

"No. No completely," she said. "No. Shut 'em down and clean them up. You are not doing this in my name, with my consent!"

The women's trial is scheduled for next week.

One hundred Canadians who call themselves the

"Raging Grannies" identify themselves from the audience, wearing straw hats covered with plastic flowers and birds. The "Clown Mother" quotes Emma Goldman: "If I can't dance—I'm not coming to your revolution."

Jerry Coates, a Maori from New Zealand, the only nuclear-free nation by legislation, proposes "Operation Gridlock," suggesting we drive the minimum speed limit on all federal interstates. And then Jackie Cabassco, director of the Western States Legal Foundation, says, "As long as we keep testing weapons, we are engaged in nuclear war."

Corbin Harney rises to pray once again, lights the peace pipe, smokes it, then hands it to Suleimenov, who does the same.

Richard is very quiet. I wonder what his thoughts are. We are invited to participate in an ancient Russian custom: "throwing rocks at evil." Each person takes a stone and places it in a pile.

"It starts small," says Suleimenov. "But one day this mountain of stones will close this test site."

Lynne, Steve, and I pick up stones by our feet and quietly add ours to the pile. Richard stands on the periphery of the crowd. A news reporter from Salt Lake City recognizes him.

"Senator Tempest, I didn't expect to see you here."

My uncle smiles. "I'm here with my daughter and niece."

Lynne and I listen to the conversation from afar. A cameraman joins the reporter.

"Senator Tempest, would you like to make a comment on today's demonstration?"

"I would.

"Our family has been ravaged by cancer. Like many Utahns, I have chosen to ignore the facts surrounding radioactive fallout. I have just recently become a grandfather. I want to leave my little granddaughter, Hannah, a more peaceful world, if I possibly can. It was my generation who started this nuclear madness. Maybe it's up to my generation to stop it."

He pauses, unexpectedly gripped by emotion. The cameraman looks up, then stops filming.

"That's all I have to say."

January 6, 1991

BUSH TO SADDAM: PULL OUT OR ELSE

Washington, D.C.—President Bush said Saturday that his Secretary of State will forego secret diplomacy this week to demand that occupying Iraqi troops leave Kuwait "or face terrible consequences."

The President, in a hard-line radio address to the nation, issued his ultimatum that Iraqi President Saddam Hussein pull his troops out or face U.S. forces in battle.

"Time is running out," the President said. "It's running out because each day that passes brings real costs, as Saddam continues developing his nuclear capability, entrenches his troops in Kuwait and disrupts the worldwide flow of oil."

A conference to amend the Limited Test Ban Treaty of 1963 into a comprehensive test ban is to be held in New York City from January 7 to January 18, 1991, at the United Nations. The Nuclear Test Ban Conference is the culmination of more than five years of effort by six nonaligned nuclear states. Their governments understood that, without a comprehensive test ban, there could be no end to the nuclear arms race or to nuclear proliferation, and no hope for real progress toward the ultimate goal of eliminating all nuclear weapons. In addition, these six initiators of the amendment conference (Indonesia, Mexico, Peru, Sri Lanka, Venezuela, and Yugoslavia) were fed up with the procrastination of the three nuclear powers and their endless specious arguments for not ending underground testing.

The USSR supports the amendment proposal, but the United States and Britain announced they will veto the amendment and described the conference as a waste of time and money.

January 10, 1991

U.S., IRAQ MOVE A STEP CLOSER TO WAR

Geneva—The United States and Iraq moved to the threshold of war Wednesday when talks between Secretary James Baker and Iraqi Foreign Minister Tariq Aziz failed to resolve any aspect of the five-month-old Persian Gulf crisis.

President Bush, declaring he was "discouraged by Iraq's total stiff arm," said he would continue to seek peace.

Last night, Peter Matthiessen gave a reading at the American Museum of Natural History. He said the American psyche that wants war is the same psyche that doesn't want wilderness.

"It's about an empathetic intelligence," he said. "Issues of peace and issues of the environment are rooted in a sacredness of life."

Throughout New York, I hear nothing but conversations of war. Riding up the elevator to meet with my editor, I hear two young delivery men discussing the Gulf crisis.

"What do you think we should do?" I ask.

"Kick butt," one answers.

"Saddam is Hitler," the other responds.

"Would you go and fight?" I ask.

The elevator stops. The doors open.

"In a flash."

On the bus to the United Nations, I read Diane di Prima's poem "Rant":

> The only war that matters is the war
>   against the imagination

The only war that matters is the war
      against the imagination
The only war that matters is the war
      against the imagination
All other wars are subsumed in it.

I look up, but the bus windows are fogged. I cannot see out. I wonder how I will know when to get off.

It is raining. Each night from 5:00 until 6:30 P.M., a candlelight vigil is held across the street from the United Nations at Isaiah's Wall.

Tonight, there are two of us. Our hands try to shield the small flames of our candles.

"Are you crazy?" asks a trench-coated man as he briskly waves down a cab. "Where are you from?"

"Utah," I answer.

"Utah? And why are you standing in the god-awful weather?"

"To support the amendment of the partial test ban treaty to full nuclear test ban," the other woman replies.

"Jesus," he says as he collapses his black umbrella and slides into a cab. "Don't you girls know we're about to go to war? Who gives a damn about a test ban treaty?"

A Patriot's Journal

January 11, 1991

CONGRESS SCRAMBLES TO AUTHORIZE WAR

Washington, D.C.——Congress on Thursday sped toward its starkest war-and-peace decision since World War II, and leaders in both parties predicted President Bush would get what he wants: authority to take the nation to war in the Persian Gulf.

Sen. John Danforth, R-Mo., said it would be unthinkable for Congress to undercut Bush after the United States had led the international coalition against Saddam Hussein, and he contended it had become clear economic sanctions would not force Iraq out of Kuwait.

"The captain cannot abandon the ship," Danforth said. "It is not an option of the U.S. Congress to disapprove what we for months have asked others to support."

"Lies! Lies! Lies! I can take no more," shouts Rick Springer in the middle of the afternoon plenary session of the amendment conference.

Ian Kenyon, the head of the British delegation, stated: ". . . the technology for containing underground tests has reached a high degree of sophistication. As a result, the problem of environmental damage at the site where we test has been minimized . . . all radioactive releases since 1970 could not have posed a threat to public health."

"Lies! Lies! Lies!" Springer cries. Suddenly, a chant of hand claps rises from the gallery, while at the same time, a number of British conferees stand up and turn their backs in protest of Kenyon.

The plenary session is suspended.

January 12, 1991

It is after 6 P.M. Dark. A crowd of around three hundred has gathered across from the United Nations. We are standing vigil once again. Each of us holds a poster-size photograph of a nuclear blast. Mine is number 505, Operation Knox, 8.7 times the force of Hiroshima, detonated on February 21, 1968, at the Nevada test site. I was twelve years old.

January 15, 1991

U.S. AND IRAQ STAND ON THE BRINK OF WAR
Washington, D.C.—Last-ditch peace efforts appear doomed as France offered a last-minute proposal Monday to avert war in the Persian Gulf, but the United States appeared to reject the plan because it called for talks on the Palestinian question in exchange for Iraq's pullout from Kuwait.

Home in Salt Lake City, I have brought back mementos for my nieces, Sara and Callie, who are five and eight. A man I had met in New York had taken small black film canisters and put a paper banner around them that read NO BLOOD FOR OIL, with a place to write your name and address and mail to George Bush. All it required to get to the White House was forty-five cents' postage.

"A political recycling project," the old man had said. I brought home a handful.

I ring the doorbell. The girls throw open the door, hug me, and exclaim, "Look, Terry, did you see our new flag?"

I hadn't noticed it waving above the porch. Red, white, and blue. I quietly put the black canisters in my pocket.

January 16, 1991

It is the anniversary of Mother's death. Four years. Cancer. Our family—my father, grandfather, three brothers, and I—have agreed to meet at her grave at 5:15 P.M.

I order a bouquet of birds-of-paradise, her favorite flowers. I pick them up at Mildred's Floral Shop. She remembers Mother and knows they are for her.

Driving into the cemetery, I am listening to National Public Radio. It is five o'clock. The news changes abruptly. We have bombed Baghdad. America is at war.

Each of us arrives at Mother's grave. Each of us

has heard the news. We are startled and shocked. I get out of my car carrying the birds-of-paradise. Steve arrives. Dan. Hank. Jack, our grandfather. Dad has his back to us as he is shoveling the snow off his wife's grave. When the bronze plaque that bears her name, DIANE DIXON TEMPEST, MARCH 7, 1932—JANUARY 16, 1987, is exposed, he turns around and faces us.

He is crying.

"Why? When we know the pain and suffering of one individual and what death means to a family, why would we purposefully choose to inflict death on all these Iraqi families through war?"

We gather around him and stand on the parameters of the grave. I lay the tropical flowers on top of the snow. No one speaks. We all weep—not for Mother.

There was nothing we could do but stand together in silence, watching the sun set over the Oquirrh Mountains and cast a red winter alpenglow east across the Wasatch Range.

January 17, 1991

WAR EXPLODES IN THE GULF

Washington, D.C.—The United States and its allies went to war Wednesday night against Iraq, battering Baghdad with wave after wave of fighter bombers in hope of routing Iraq from occupied Kuwait.

President Bush, declared, "The world could wait no longer."

My cousin, Scott Dixon, is in Saudi Arabia. He is fluent in Arabic and was deployed the last week of August as a linguistic specialist to assist the ground troops. He left a wife and two children at home.

I call my aunt in Provo, Utah, to see if she has heard from him.

Indeed, she has.

"Scott called us about three o'clock this morning," she says. "He just returned from a two-week helicopter tour where his assignment was to locate caravans of Bedouins who were inside the fire arenas in danger of meeting loose artillery. They would locate these nomads in the desert, their camels, their tents, touch down, and translate in Arabic the imminence of war."

My aunt pauses.

"At one point, a woman holding a small child looked directly into Scott's eyes and asked, 'What is this you speak of and what would you have us do?' "

My aunt pauses for a second time.

"I honestly believe Scott will be fine. He is fortunate to be removed from the lines of fire. But when I asked him how he was feeling, he answered, 'Mother, tell me, how does one translate madness?' "

All That Is Hidden

I refuse to sign the "hold harmless" agreement issued by the Barry M. Goldwater Air Force Range. We need this piece of paper before legally entering the Cabeza Prieta National Wildlife Refuge, which is within the range's boundaries. The document absolves the United States government from "any claim of liability for death or injury arising out of . . . usage of, or presence upon, the said Range."

Those who sign are warned of four facts:

1. That there is "danger of injury or death due to falling objects, such as aircraft, live ammunition, or missiles."

2. That there is "danger of injury or death due to presence of not-yet-exploded live ordnance lying on or under
ground."

3. That there is "danger of injury or death from the presence of old mine shafts and other openings or weaknesses
in the earth, as well as other natural and/or man-made
conditions which are too numerous to recite."

4. That the land "cannot be feasibly marked to warn the
location and nature of each danger."

"It's a formality," my husband says. "Just sign
it." He is irritated by my unwillingness to do what we
have to do to get into beautiful country.

"It's not a formality for me," I answer. "I want
my government to be accountable."

And so I enter the Cabeza Prieta unlawfully.

I am traveling with my husband, Brooke, and
ethnobotanist Gary Nabhan. We are here to count
sheep: desert bighorn. Nothing official, simply for ourselves.

The night before, in Organ Pipe Cactus National Monument some fifty miles from the Cabeza, I
dreamt of searching for a one-eyed ram. Brooke and Gary
tease me at breakfast when I tell them of my night
image.

"Sounds phallic to me," says Brooke.

Gary offers a retort in Spanish or Papago or both
and does not translate.

In Celtic lore, the spiral horns of the ram are attributes of war gods. In Egyptian mythology, the ram is the personification of Amon-Ra, the Sun God: "Ra . . . thou ram, mightiest of created things." It is virility, the masculine generative force, the creative heat. In the Bible, it is the sacrificial animal.

Conversation shifts in base camp as we load our daypacks for a seven-mile walk to Sheep Mountain. I take two water bottles, sunblock, rain gear, a notebook and pencil, and a lunch of raisins, cream cheese, and crackers. I also slip in some lemon drops.

Gary hands Brooke and me each a black comb.

"A subtle grooming hint?" I ask.

"For cholla," he grins. "To pull the spines out of your legs when you bump into them."

We begin walking. It is early morning, deeply quiet. Each of us follows our own path in solitude, meandering through mesquite, paloverde, ocotillo, and cholla. The animated postures of the giant saguaros create a lyrical landscape, the secret narratives of desert country expressed through mime. Perhaps they will steer us toward bighorn.

Ovis canadensis. Bighorn walk on the tips of their toes. Their tracks are everywhere. In the vast silences of the Cabeza Prieta, these animals engage in panoramic pleasure; hidden on steep, rocky slopes, they miss nothing. Elusive, highly adaptive to climatic extremes, desert bighorn are graced with a biological patience when it comes to water. Research shows that bighorn here have gone without water for periods extending from July to December, maybe even longer. But most sheep find watering holes or small depressions in the rocks that hold moisture after a rain, enough to drink at least weekly.

Bones. White bones are scattered between the lava boulders. Given the terrain, tracks, and scat, it's a safe bet they're bighorn. There are ribs, vertebrae, and a pelvis that looks like a mask. Where the balls of the femurs once fit is now empty space. I see eyes. I look around—nothing stirs, with the exception of side-blotched lizards. Now you see them, now you don't.

Brooke and Gary wait ahead of me. Before I catch up to them, I see a saguaro that looks like the Reverend Mother, her arms generously calling me toward her. I come; at her feet is an offering of gilded flicker feathers.

The men tell me the sheep tank is around the next bend; according to the map, we are less than a mile away. Bighorn could be watering there.

Gary has found a pack-rat midden made out of cholla and shrapnel. He tells us how enterprising these creatures are in building their dens. "Quite simply, they use what's available," he says. The glare from the silver metal blinds us. "We can trace the history of desert vegetation in the arid Southwest through these middens," he continues, "sometimes as far back as forty thousand years. Food remains become cemented with pack-rat urine. These fecal deposits represent centuries of seed gathering."

Brooke accidentally brushes against the den as he turns to leave. He winces. A cholla hangs from his calf, spines imbedded in flesh. Out comes the comb, out come the needles. The clouds are beginning to gather and darken. Barrel cacti are blooming, blood-red.

Bighorn are tracking my imagination. I recall the last one I saw, a young ram with horns just beginning to curl. He was kneeling on wet sand as he drank from the Colorado River. His large brown eyes looked up, then down to the flowing water. In the Grand Canyon, we were no threat.

Threat. Rams. Rivals. The bighorn was the mascot of my high school. The football song comes back to me. ("Oh, the big rams are rambling, scrambling, rambling. . . .") As Pep Club president, I cut ram tracks out of black construction paper and then taped them to sidewalks leading to the front doors of athletes' homes. Where the tracks ended, we placed Rice Krispies treats with a "go-fight-win" letter wishing them luck. In the desolation of the Cabeza, I wonder how I have found my way from the pom-pom culture of Salt Lake City to this truly wild place.

No sheep tank in sight, although Sheep Mountain is. We decide to climb the ridge and eat lunch. The view will orient us and perhaps even inspire us to think like a ram.

Gary pulls out of his pack a small glass bottle filled with something resembling red beads. "Try a couple of these on your cream cheese and crackers," he says.

"What are they?" Brooke asks, taking a handful.

"Chiltepines. The Tarahumara believe they are the greatest protection against the evils of sorcery." We trust our friend and spread them on our crackers.

One bite—instant pain, red-hot and explosive. We grab water and gulp in waves, trying to douse the flames that are dancing in our throats. Gary, blue-eyed and blissful, adds more and more to his crackers. "I once ate thirty-nine chiltepines in a competition," he says nonchalantly. "In fact, in all modesty, I am the Arizona state champion." I bypass lunch altogether and suck on lemon drops, praying for a healing.

It begins to rain, lightly. As far as we can see, the desert glistens. The Growlers, jagged black peaks, carry the eye range after range into Mexico; no national boundaries exist in the land's mind. The curvature of the earth bends the horizon in an arc of light. Virga: rain evaporating in midair, creating gray-blue streamers that wave back and forth, never touching the ground. Who is witness to this full-bodied beauty? Who can withstand the recondite wisdom and sonorous silence of wildness?

All at once, a high-pitched whining shatters us, flashes over our shoulders, threatens to blow us off the ridge. Two jets scream by. Within seconds, one, two, three bombs drop. The explosions are deafening; the desert is in flames.

The bombers veer left, straight black wings perpendicular to the land, vertical rudders on either side of their tails. The double engines behind the wings look like drums. The jets roll back to center, fly low, drop two more bombs. Flames explode on the desert and then columns of smoke slowly rise like black demons.

The dark aircraft bank. I have seen them before, seabirds, parasitic jaegers that turn with the slightest dip of a wing. I am taken in by their beauty, their aerial finesse. And I imagine the pilots inside the cockpits seeing only sky from the clear plastic bubbles that float on top of the fuselage, jet jockeys with their hair on fire following only a crossline on a screen.

We are now in a cloudburst, the land, the mountains, and the aircraft disappearing in a shroud of dense clouds. Rolling thunder masks the engines and the explosions. Everything is hidden.

"Basic ground warfare. Tank busters," Technical Sergeant Richard Smith tells me. He is the spokesman for the 58th Fighter Wing at Luke Air Force Base, twenty miles west of Phoenix. "What you witnessed were Warthogs at work."

"Excuse me?"

"Warthogs, known by civilians as the Fairchild A-10 Thunderbolt II. They are extremely maneuverable machines that can stay close to their target." He pauses. "Did you watch the war?"

"Yeah, I watched the war."

"Then you saw them in action. These babies carry sixteen thousand pounds of mixed ordnance:

bombs, rockets, missiles, laser-guided bombs, and bullets. They are specifically designed to destroy enemy tanks, and they do. Twenty-three hundred Iraqi vehicles were knocked out during Desert Storm."

"And what we saw below Sheep Mountain?"

"Mock air-to-surface missile strikes. Some twenty to thirty aircraft use the South Tactical Range each day. This is a 'live fire' area where we train our pilots. It has been since the 1940s."

"Has any ordnance accidentally been dropped on the refuge?"

"Never."

"And how do the jets and noise affect the bighorn sheep?"

"They don't."

Not everyone would agree. Monte Dodson of the U.S. Fish and Wildlife Service maintains that "bighorn continually exposed to sonic booms, as on the Cabeza Prieta Wildlife Refuge in Arizona, may develop severe stress problems that inhibit normal daily living patterns, as well as reproduction."

What I know as a human being standing on the ridge of Sheep Mountain on the edge of the Cabeza Prieta National Wildlife Refuge is that primal fear shot through my bones. In that moment, I glimpsed war.

Instead of counting sheep, I am counting bombs. The A-10s that swept the sky at high noon are gone. F-16s have taken over. They are silver and sleek. I will learn from Sergeant Smith that these are one-person, single-engine aircraft designed for air-to-air attack, hence the nickname "Fighting Falcon." Like the peregrine, speed is their virtue. Five hundred miles per hour is a usual clip. The F-15E, also employed above the Cabeza, is a two-person, double-engine jet capable of defending itself air-to-air as well as air-to-ground. It is known to intimates as the "Strike Eagle." Lying on my back with binoculars pointed up, I realize that I am engaged in military ornithology.

Four jets screech above me, and every cell in my body contracts. I am reduced to an animal vulnerability. They can do with me what they wish: one button, I am dead. I am a random target with the cholla, ocotillo, lizards, and ants. In the company of orange-and-black-beaded gila monsters, I am expendable. No, it's worse than that—we do not exist.

Over the ridge, bombs batter the desert. The ghosts of war walk across the bajada. I imagine their grief-stricken faces, gaunt, cheated. Bombs counted: 23. Sheep counted: 0.

We have dropped down from the pass. Gary and Brooke continue hiking up-canyon; I choose to sit near a windmill where there is a cistern of water, still hopeful for a look at desert bighorn.

More jets, more bombs: the machinery of freedom. I scan the hillside with my binoculars. The small black boulders are covered with petroglyphs; the etched images are pink. I walk across the wash for a closer look. Miniature rock murals are everywhere. Who were these artists, these scribes? When were they here? And what did they witness? Time has so little meaning in the center of the desert. The land holds a collective memory in the stillness of open spaces. Perhaps our only obligation is to listen and remember.

Bighorn. I walk toward him, stoop down, and run my fingers over the primitive outline of his stone body. Wavy lines run out from the hooves like electrical currents. This ram is very old, his horns spiral close to a circle like moons on either side of his head. And then I stand up, step back. This stone sheep has one eye.

Night in the Cabeza restores silence to the desert, that holy, intuitive silence. No more jets. No more bombs. Not even an owl or a coyote. Above me is an ocean of stars, and I wonder how it is that in the midst of wild serenity we as a species choose to shatter it again and again. Silence is our national security, our civil defense. By destroying silence, the legacy of our deserts, we leave no room for peace, the deep peace that elevates and stirs our souls. It is silence that rocks and awakens us to the truth of our dreams.

Tonight in the Cabeza Prieta, I feel the eyes of the desert bighorn. It is I who am being watched. It is I who am being counted.

Testimony

BEFORE THE
SUBCOMMITTEE ON FISHERIES AND WILDLIFE
CONSERVATION AND THE ENVIRONMENT
CONCERNING
THE PACIFIC YEW ACT OF 1991

MS. WILLIAMS: Thank you, Mr. Chairman and subcommittee members. I appreciate being able to testify on behalf of Pacific yew management. My name is Terry Tempest Williams. I come to you as a woman concerned about health. I am thirty-six years old. I am the matriarch of my family. Nine women in my family have had mastectomies. Seven are dead. My mother passed away from ovarian cancer in 1987. We have had subsequent deaths in 1988, 1989, and 1990. I am aware of the intimate, painful struggle of women, families, and cancer.

Testimony

Taxus brevifolia, Pacific yew. Fossil records of this evergreen tree have been found and placed within the Jurassic Era, 140 billion years ago. Ironically, our federal government, the National Forest Service, and the Bureau of Land Management have viewed the Pacific yew as a trash tree, a nuisance, a weed to get out of the way so they can manage and perpetuate the clearcut technology that supports the harvesting of Douglas fir. *Taxus brevifolia's* most current habitat has been slash piles.

Up until now, nobody cared. The yew was invisible, expendable. But the story has changed. The status of the Pacific yew has been raised. The yew tree contains taxol, which has been proven to be an effective treatment against ovarian and breast cancers. We know this narrative through the National Cancer Institute, through Bristol-Myers, through the National Forest Service, the BLM, and conservation groups. What don't we know?

I can tell you that my mother, who had ovarian cancer, didn't know she had any more options after a radical hysterectomy, Cytoxan, cisplatin, Adriamycin treatments, and six weeks of radiation therapy had failed to offer her a cure. Pacific yew, *Taxus brevifolia*, taxol were not words in her vocabulary, or in her doctor's vocabulary for that matter. I remember the day in June when her doctor said, "Diane, I am sorry. We have done all we can do for you. My advice to you is to go home, get your life in order, and enjoy the time you have left." My mother died six months later, a woman fifty-four years old. My grandmothers and aunts are also dead—breast cancer. They didn't know they had taxol options either. But my grandmother did know about yew trees. She loved them. They formed the hedge around her home, and she knew them as a mythical tree, telling us as children that in England they were planted on the graves of our English ancestors. Their roots would wind their ways into the mouths of the dead and give them eternal voice. And on long summer nights we imagined hearing the voices of our dead singing across the continents, whispering through the hedges of yew, coming back to us. As a Mormon girl in Utah, I believed this.

In anticipation of today's hearing on the management of the Pacific yew, I traveled last month to the Willamette National Forest in Oregon and the checkerboard BLM lands in the largest timber-producing forest in the United States. As a woman with a strong family history of both ovarian and breast cancer, I wanted to see wild Pacific yew for myself. I want to believe I have options for my future so when my oncologist says to me as he has, "It is not if you get cancer, but when," I can hold on to the boughs of this healing tree.

I stepped into Lane County. I was not prepared for what I saw.

Site One: the Getting Conference Timber Sale. My guide was David Hale, professional woodcutter, who lives in Cottage Grove, Oregon. He is a scavenger. He makes his living off the slash piles of clearcuts. A clearcut.

Testimony

It has always been an abstraction to me. My friend Sandra Lopez, a resident of Lane County, from the McKenzie River valley, created a broadside titled "Clearcut." I would like to add this to the *Congressional Record.* She wanted to express what she saw—the clearcuts around her home. Sandra printed the text of the 23rd Psalm, "The Lord is my shepherd . . ." You open the book and the sacred text has been mutilated. She removed individual words and passages with an X-acto knife. Clearcut.

Clearcut. The Getting Conference Timber Sale. BLM lands. The Bohemia Timber Company all involved. David Hale had a permit to cut firewood. What he found was sixty yew trees in the slash—sixty dead, mutilated yew trees unmarked, unpeeled—wasted trees. According to the National Cancer Institute, the yew tree grows so slowly that it takes the bark of three hundred-year-old trees to treat a single cancer patient. Sixty yew trees divided by three—we are talking twenty women who could have been treated with taxol. My mother? My grandmothers? My aunts? Your mother? Your wife? Twenty women. Sixty trees lying dead on top of the clearcut with limbs and needles still intact.

David Hale blew the whistle. The BLM said David Hale couldn't identify yew. He couldn't tell them apart from cedar. What we found was that the BLM couldn't tell the difference. May I submit to the subcommittee branches mistaken for yew: Douglas fir painted blue. Wrong. And here is vine maple painted blue, also identified as Pacific yew. Wrong. I would like to enter these specimens for the record.

On January 20, 1992, David Hale found sixty full yew trees among the slash. He figured that there were at least two hundred cords of good firewood available, worth close to ten thousand dollars for his income. On January 25, 1992, five days later, same site, same slash pile, the Bohemia Timber Company had bulldozed the slash, not only destroying most of the Pacific yew trees but hiding them beneath the cedars at the bottom of the pile, a nasty cover-up. David Hale has a video to document this illegal act. I urge the committee to secure it for themselves as evidence of this tragic waste of yew. I have submitted his address in my formal testimony.

The irony here is that if David Hale were to strip one piece of yew bark, he would be fined ten thousand dollars. But if left in the slash pile, he can cut it as firewood. Clearcut. BLM. Business as usual. Douglas firs are of value. Pacific yews are not. Ladies and gentlemen, nothing has changed in the mind of our federal government. Our healing options, the gift of the Pacific yew, are going up in smoke. As I left, David pointed me to a burned hillside. He figured he watched fifty thousand cords of wood burn, and he said, "In every old-growth slash pile, there are Pacific yew."

Site Two: Lost Horizon Timber Sale. I traveled to the back of Mount June. BLM lands once again. This time my companions were Dick Wilcox and Dave Barton, professional yew-bark collectors of NaPro, a private company interested in securing taxol not only from the bark but from the needles as well. Wilcox and Barton told me they had harvested six hundred pounds of dry yew bark from this site. When I got there, I was stunned. The hillside was charred. The BLM's definition: a broadcast burn. The taxol molecule is destroyed at 150°F. Dick said it is not worth collecting. They figured they lost six hundred more pounds of taxol. That translates to ten grams of taxol, five women, five more women who were not treated.

In conclusion, the web of life in the Pacific Northwest is rapidly unraveling. We are seeing ourselves as part of the fabric. It is not a story about us versus them. That is too easy. It is not a story to pit conservationists against cancer patients. That is too easy also. Nor is it a story about corporate greed against a free-market economy. It is a story about healing and how we might live with hope.

The poet W. S. Merwin says, "I want to tell what the forests were like. I will have to speak a forgotten language." I am asking you as members of this subcommittee, as my lawmakers, my guardians of justice, for one favor. Will you please go visit the trees? See them for yourself—these beautiful healing trees growing wildly, mysteriously, in the draws of our ancient forests, and then go visit the adjacent clearcuts, walk among the wreckage, the slash piles, forage through the debris, and look again for the Pacific yew. Think about health. Think about the women you love—our bodies, the land—and think about what was once rich and dense and green with standing. Think about how our sacred texts may be found in the forest as well as in the Psalms, and then, my dear lawmakers, I ask you to make your decision with your heart, what you felt in the forest in the presence of a forgotten language.

And if you cannot make a decision from this place of heart, from this place of compassionate intelligence, we may have to face as a people the horror of this nation, that our government and its leaders are heartless.

The Wild Card

Where do our preoccupations lie as women?

Our home is being held in the arms of angels as it snows and snows and snows, and throughout these winter days I hold the questions of a woman's life in my bones. Quiet days. Days sitting by the fire. Days walking, sleeping, and dreaming. I see myself slowing down and moving away from a darkened state. The Winter Solstice becomes my own. I allow myself to struggle with the obligations of a public life and the spiritual necessity for a private one.

The Wild Card

Am I an activist or an artist?

Do I stay home or do I speak out?

When Edward Abbey calls for the artist to be a critic of his or her society, do we live on the page or do we live in the world?

It just may be that the most radical act we can commit is to stay home. Otherwise, who will be there to chart the changes? Who will be able to tell us if the long-billed curlews have returned to the grassy vales of Promontory, Utah? Who will be there to utter the cry of loss when the salmon of the McKenzie River in Oregon are nowhere to be seen?

Claudine Herrmann writes in *The Tongue Snatchers*: "The beauty of the world, the health of its creatures, the emotion of love, and the thirst for justice are sacrificed every day to the will of power, and it astonishes me that all political systems, no matter how different they appear, end up with the same singular result: that of placing life last among all their preoccupations."

Where are our preoccupations as women?

Perhaps here: It would begin with each woman carrying a deck of cards—wild cards—cards that could not only portend the future but create it. If a woman saw an act that violated the health and integrity of her community, she would leave a card on-site. If she was moved by a particular piece of legislation on behalf of or against the land, she would dash a card off to her senator or representative. And if she found herself in a board of directors meeting and the truth as she felt it was not being told, she would place all her cards on the table as a sign that the games of men are not the games of women.

And here: As Americans, we have always left when the land became degraded, moved on to the next best place. Walked west. Now, our continent is inhabited. There is no place left to go. What would happen, then, if we took the Homestead Act of 1862, designed to open the West to settlement by small family farms in 160-acre parcels, and turned it inside out, reimagined and reshaped it to meet the needs of our own time? We could call it the Home Stand Act of 1994, designed to inspire and initiate a community of vigilance and care toward the lands we inhabit. It would give us courage to honor "the stay option" and dig in, set down roots. A Home Stand Act placed in the hands of women and their families could activate a local force so brilliant and full-spirited it could bypass traditional forms of government altogether. The artistry, intelligence, and compassion of women would flow through our communities like water.

Within Mormon culture, there is an organization of women known as the Relief Society. Organized in 1852, its charge is to attend to the needs of the community. The Relief Society, like other church auxiliaries, provides opportunities for association, leadership, compassionate service, and education. Its motto, "Charity Never Faileth," expresses the commitment of members to love and nurture one another, neighbor to neighbor, household to household, ministering graciously to the needs of others.

The Relief Society was a constant source of comfort in our home as I was growing up in Salt Lake City. Two Mormon sisters were "called" to watch over our family. They visited us monthly, anticipating whatever needs we might have. And when our mother became ill, they not only stayed with us while she was in the hospital but provided meals for us, talked to us, and held us in their prayers. They rendered peace throughout our lives. Again, as I was growing up, I often witnessed casserole diplomacy being exercised in our neighborhood. Food was brought into homes to heal the sick, mend a feud, or welcome a new baby into the world. Personal offerings dissolved political boundaries. I believe the idea of the Home Stand Act could incorporate this kind of community care and awareness, because it has everything to do with home rule: standing our ground in the places we love. This is the wild card we hold, and if we choose to adopt a Home Stand Act, nothing will escape our green eyes.

There are role models among us. Wangari Maathai founded the Green Belt Movement in Kenya, Africa, by planting seven trees on June 5, 1977. "The Green Belt Movement started in my backyard," she writes in her essay "Foresters Without Diplomas." "I became exposed to many of the problems women were facing—problems of firewood, malnutrition, lack of food and adequate water, unemployment, soil erosion . . . so we went to the women and talked about planting trees and overcoming, for example, such problems as the lack of firewood and building and fencing materials, stopping soil erosion, protecting water systems. . . . The women agreed."

It was an arduous, labor-intensive process. "To initiate the campaign," Aubrey Wallace writes in *Eco-Heroes*, "Maathai went into the schools." The children were involved directly: they dug holes, walked to the tree nursery to collect trees, planted them, and took care of them as long as they were in school. "It was the children who took the message home to their parents and eventually got women's groups interested," says Maathai.

Sixteen years later, more than three thousand schools have responded to the Green Belt campaign, with over 1 million children involved. More than 10 million trees stand throughout Kenya, with over 1,500 nurseries, virtually all of them operated by women.

I met Wangari Maathai in Nairobi in August 1985, at the United Nations Decade for Women. She took me into the countryside to see for myself how rural women in Africa were gathering indigenous seeds in the folds of their skirts. I remember her picking up a handful of red soil. "The weight of the environmental crisis that rural women have been carrying on their backs is being lessened," she said, "one seed at a time."

In our own country, we only have to look to Rachel Carson to see the impact one woman can have.

The Wild Card

Carson received a burning letter from her friend Olga Owens Huckins, a journalist, who asked her for help in finding people who could elucidate and speak to the dangers of pesticides. The Huckinses had a small place in Duxbury, Massachusetts, just north of Cape Cod, which they had transformed into a bird sanctuary. Without any thought of the effects on birds and wildlife, the state had sprayed the entire area for mosquito control.

Huckins sent a letter of outrage to the *Boston Herald* in January 1958. An excerpt:

The mosquito control plane flew over our small town last summer. Since we live close to the marshes, we were treated to several lethal doses as the pilot crisscrossed our place. And we consider the spraying of active poison over private land to be a serious aerial intrusion.

The "harmless" shower bath killed seven of our lovely songbirds outright. We picked up three dead bodies the next morning right by the door. They were birds that lived close to us, trusted us, and built their nests in our trees year after year. The next day three were scattered around the bird bath. (I had emptied it and scrubbed it after the spraying but YOU CAN NEVER KILL D.D.T.). . . . All of these birds died horribly and in the same way. Their bills were gaping open, and their splayed claws were drawn up to their breasts in agony.

Olga Owens Huckins bore witness. Rachel Carson responded. A correspondence between friends. Two women. Carson wrote to Huckins that it was her letter that had "started it all" and had led her to realize that "I must write the book."

Four and a half years later, *Silent Spring* was published and alerted the world of 1962 to the dangers of pesticides when they enter the food chain. Nothing exists in isolation. The metaphor of silence—birdsong lost forever as a result of chemical pollutants—shot through the conservation community like a wave of electricity. Letters were written. Commissions were formed. Laws were enacted. A new wave of environmentalism began.

And then in 1975, Lois Gibbs brought the issue of toxic wastes into the mainstream of American culture, when she began to speak out against the twenty-two thousand tons of poisons that were "bubbling underground" in the Love Canal neighborhood of Niagara Falls, New York. Cancers, miscarriages, illnesses, and death among the children and adults of the Niagara River valley were being linked to the poisons. Lois Gibbs responded with a community program, the Citizens' Clearing House for Hazardous Wastes. "If they didn't have a sense of community prior to our proposal, they developed it as a result," she said of her neighbors. "It's one issue that can bring all different people together."

Women, health, and the environment. Home rule. The Home Stand Act. We can create beauty through the dailiness of our lives, standing our ground in the places we love. "There is a real world that is really dying," Marilynne Robinson writes in *Mother Country*, "and we had better think about that. My greatest hope, which is a very slender one, is that we will at last find the courage to make ourselves rational and morally autonomous adults, secure enough in the faith that life is good and to be preserved, to recognize the grosser forms of evil and name them and confront them. Who will do it for us?"

We must do it for ourselves.

As women wedded to wilderness, we must realize that we do carry the wild card, that our individual voices matter and our collective voice can shatter the status quo that for too long has legislated on behalf of power and far too little on behalf of life. We can flood Congress with our wild cards (imagine hundreds of thousands of brightly colored cards covering the desks of our representatives), demanding that women's issues be recognized as health issues, as environmental issues, as issues centered around a quality of life that touches all of us, deeply. This is the kind of politics we must be engaged in—nothing marginal, nothing peripheral, nothing inessential, not anymore.

As women within the conservation community, we must work tirelessly to see that the staffs, boards of directors, and governing councils of environmental organizations in this country carry a fair representation of women and minorities. We must call for the abandonment of hierarchies that contribute to the vertical power that has compromised the earth. And we must begin to build broad coalitions and alliances, just as Elaine R. Jones, leader of the NAACP Legal Defense and Educational Fund, has promised to do by expanding its civil rights agenda to include more cases of environmental and health-care discrimination.

"We, as women," Chantal Chawaf writes in *Shifting Scenes: Interviews on Women, Writing, and Politics in Post-'68 France,* "today, in our logos and discourse, have to articulate the excess desire, the uncensored body, and life—not an idealized life, but life just as it is, with its problems, anxieties, and frightening aspects. We must do so because it is precisely this fear of life that has kept life outside culture."

It will not be simple.

It will not be fast.

It will be a slow, steady river that braids our communities together.

Home. It continues to snow. My dreams of angels disappear and I think about the wild cards we carry, one by one, flashing the face of Eve on this creation.

Redemption

For Wendell Berry

Driving toward Malheur Lake in the Great Basin of southeastern Oregon, I saw a coyote. I stopped the car, opened the door, and walked toward him.

It was another crucifixion in the West, a hide hung on a barbed-wire fence with a wrangler's prayer: Cows are sacred. Sheep, too. No trespassing allowed. The furred skin was torn with ragged edges, evidence that it had been pulled away from the dog-body by an angry hand and a dull knife.

Redemption

Standing in the middle of the High Desert, cumulus clouds pulled my gaze upward. I thought about Coyote Butte, a few miles south, how a person can sit on top between two sage-covered ears and watch a steady stream of western tanagers fly through during spring migration; yellow bodies, black wings, red heads.

And how a few miles west near Foster Flats, one can witness dancing grouse on their ancestral leks, even in rain, crazy with desire, their booming breasts mimicking the sound of water.

Down the road, I watched a small herd of pronghorn on the other side of the fence, anxiously running back and forth parallel to the barbed wire, unable to jump. Steens Mountain shimmered above the sage flats like a ghost.

My eyes returned to Jesus Coyote, stiff on his cross, savior of our American rangelands. We can try and kill all that is native, string it up by its hind legs for all to see, but spirit howls and wildness endures.

Anticipate resurrection.

About the Author

Terry Tempest Williams lives in Salt Lake City, Utah, with her husband, Brooke. She is the author of *Pieces of White Shell: A Journey to Navajoland* (1984), *Coyote's Canyon* (1989), and two children's books. Her most recent book is *Refuge: An Unnatural History of Family and Place*, which chronicles the rise of the Great Salt Lake and the death of her mother from ovarian cancer. She is the recipient of the 1993 Lannen Literary Fellowship for nonfiction.

Terry Tempest Williams is Naturalist-in-Residence at the Utah Museum of Natural History.